BLIND DATES

GRACE OTHERWISE • VOLUME 1

HARAMBEE K. GREY-SUN

HYPERVERSE BOOKS, LLC

Cover design by Kelvin Reese

Cover art copyright © Chainat | Dreamstime.com

Published by HyperVerse Books, LLC

PO Box 23642, Alexandria, VA 22304

www.hyperversebooks.com

Crossing genres without apologies.

Print ISBN-13: 978-1-64044-023-4

Ebook ISBN-13: 978-1-64044-024-1

CONTENTS

ACKNOWLEDGMENTS

Grateful acknowledgment is made to the editors and publishers of *The Arcanist*, where "Violets Are Cruel" first appeared.

BEHOLDER

"Let's weigh my sins against yours."

Intriguing, Wayne thought. And certainly not the words he expected a woman to say after ordering drinks on a first date—but Nayantara was nothing if not bold. Wayne respected that. Heck, he respected any woman who had the audacity to challenge him to a blind date.

It could never be anything less than a challenge. He knew what he had going for him: an easy-on-the-eyes, white-collar marketing professional living in Washington, DC—a popular city teeming with transient women, most of whom were either bright-eyed grads venturing out on their first careers or bleary-eyed, estranged singles making sincere but clumsy attempts to start their lives over.

Hell, he'd have had his pick of the fruit even if he hadn't been kid-free, disease-free, and wife-free—the Big Three desirables of would-be sweeties looking to get themselves attached.

A popular assumption was that fit and reasonably attractive folks in their early twenties had it made. Most women probably did. But men who could maintain their looks and physique up through their late thirties without accumulating any baggage-with-handles were the real golden targets. Some professional women liked their men older; some liked them younger. Wayne was at just the right age to have his pick from the patch of those in their twenties and early thirties and the orchard of those in their forties and early fifties. Every now and then, he'd pluck something intriguingly mysterious that would turn out to have no more potential than black licorice—the generic, dollar-store kind. But he could already see there was nothing generic about Nayantara. She'd do for tonight. All he had to do was get her onto his field.

She'd extended the hand. He'd extend his in turn and *pull*.

"My only sin," he said with a smirk, "is that I'm too generous. I too freely *give* of myself."

"So you want me to pick up the tab?" She gave him a sly smile. "I wouldn't want you to find yourself outspent before dessert."

He contorted his smirk into a slyer smile and leaned forward. "Depends on what you plan on ordering."

"Meat. And more meat."

"A hefty ambition to devour for such a petite woman."

She shook her head. "I don't plan to keep it inside me all that long."

He straightened in his chair. *Where the hell's the waiter?* Wayne needed his drink—badly. He'd pulled the girl onto his field without realizing he hadn't yet been ready to play—not with one of this caliber, at least. This wasn't some naïve college girl. One false move, one slip of the tongue that showed her he wasn't up to her level, and the date was over.

His male friends—the blunt ones—called it *jerk-twerking*, but Wayne refused to accept any label for his verbal style of pitching woo and taking his dues. He wasn't so audacious to consider himself a poet—not one on the level of a Willie Shakespeare anyway. But he knew how to lay those glistening earworms. He could guide the flow of his words and body language while studying the disposition of the recipient and adjusting tones and movements as necessary. A master of interpretation, he could utter the same sweet nothings to three different women and know—while speaking—whether one took it as a sly sexual come-on, an aw-shucks deprecation, or a devastating insult.

Nayantara had him at a disadvantage. She seemed to be doing much better at interpreting him than the other way around. Part of the problem was that he wasn't yet certain of his endgame, and that was usually decided shortly after first sight. Did he want to bed her, outright dump her, or keep her at arm's length as an occasional nightclub and dinner partner?

"All quiet on the western side of the table?" Nayantara asked. "I hope I didn't offend you—*BigW*."

He managed a grin. "You know, 'BigW' was just a username. You really can call me Wayne."

"Oh?" she said. "And what if I still plan on using you?"

She kept her smile, and he struggled to keep his as he examined her face, studying her expression, lingering on those enticing eyes. What was she thinking? The sportive nudging had passed into friendly tussle territory far too early. They hadn't even settled on appetizers.

He had to step back off the field and reassess . . .

Hell, maybe he had to step away momentarily from the idea of *fields*.

He wasn't a player. Not really. He just seemed like one in the eyes of lazy observers. In reality—a reality only he really saw clearly and understood—he was more like a grand gardener, one who was ineluctably drawn to cultivate and experience the entire variety of women—all possible and available women—and dig deep enough within them to find that special seed—the one that made them *them*—before cracking it open, letting it rapidly flower for him as they peeled away from themselves and into him, captivated, gushing, and spilling that sweet nectar.

These sweet-smelling mushy fruits, messy on the inside with bruised skin on the outside . . . He had the magic touch to turn them into delectable candies—sweeties forever stuck on him—at his beck and call whenever he needed them. At least until they lost their flavor and he was forced to extrude.

He delighted in testing his abilities on a wide variety of women on the spectrum. Younger, older, upper class, disadvantaged, Asian, Brazilian, Nigerian, Icelandic—name it and he'd probably dated it, working hard on at least five different fruit fleshes a week. And after taking his annual one-month hiatus, he started all over again.

This evening, it was a thirty-year-old who lived in Silver Spring, Maryland, but who had originally hailed from India. The daughter of a former diplomat, she'd come to the country and worked hard enough to earn a PhD and attain the position of ethics department head at one of the local hospitals. That's all Wayne remembered from ten paragraphs of information. After she'd initiated contact online, he'd only skimmed the text in her online dating profile while paying the bulk of his attention to her pictures. They'd been crisp, clear, full-color body shots. Her face had been blurred out in every single one, but her body had been beyond delightful.

Nayantara was impossibly but truly both petite *and* voluptuous. She obviously worked hard to maintain her curves, and she wore clothing that, while tasteful, also made sure onlookers could discern she was soft in all the right places and firm in all the others. Her face had undoubtedly been blurred for safety reasons—a smart tactic to ward off stalkers, nothing more. Wayne had figured there was no way a woman with such a sublime body could have had a face too far below average; the odds had been too much against it. So why had she reached out to *him* of all people?

He'd described himself accurately but briefly in his profile and had included no pictures. His perpetual status was that of watcher and cultivator. He wouldn't bury himself in dirt and expose his face like some unprotected plum in the sun. But after Nayantara had reached out and the two of them had engaged in a one-day exchange of emails brief enough to qualify as haiku, he'd agreed to meet her. And when they met, he'd seen that she was stunning beyond belief from bottom to top and side to side. Her eyes in particular. Something about those amber irises seemed to grab his attention and hold it for longer than any other part of her body.

At first sight, they'd exchanged the usual first-date pleasantries. Now, he was speechless, still lingering on those ravishing eyes.

The waiter delivered a much-needed intervention with their glasses of wine. Shiraz for him. Malbec for her.

"Uh, come back in five," Wayne said when the waiter raised his eyebrows. "We should be ready to order by then."

"Dessert and all," Nayantara added with a wink.

Wayne raised his glass as the waiter left. "Cheers."

They clinked, then sipped.

His wine tasted like cough syrup, and his expression showed it.

"Would you like to switch?" Nayantara asked.

"I don't think you'd like this," he said. "I'll just order another. I'm sure it'll be gratis."

"Here."

She took his glass and set hers in its place.

"It's not so bad," she said after tasting the Shiraz. "The higher-end wines from certain regions of Australia tend to be a bit thick; they weigh heavy with black fruits. Definitely fruit forward, but they sometimes give you too much to think about too soon."

Wayne tried the Malbec and found it to his liking. "Well versed in wines?"

"One of my heftier sins," Nayantara said with a nod and another wink. "I spend a bit too much on it. When I take a vacation, it's always to some country's wine region. Not a weekend goes by without me attending at least one high-end tasting in the area. I can never get enough of the variety. Take two winemakers and give them one grape—say, Shiraz—and let them play with it. The resulting wines will inevitably be different—probably *very* different—due to the variances of terroir, climate, the techniques or lack thereof of the farmers tending the vines, everything that goes into the vinification process, steel barrels, oak barrels, French oak, American oak, Hungarian, Belcharian . . ."

Wayne laughed and took another sip of the Malbec. "*This* is your sin? Oenophilia? You had me on the run, lady. I was thinking you'd chase me into dirtier territory."

She smiled. "Plenty of time for that later. For now, I'll simply venture onto soupier ground."

Wayne cocked his head and began to ask for clarification, but the waiter returned. True to her odd words, Nayantara ordered the soup of the day. Wayne ordered the sautéed mush-rooms. The waiter took the hint—Nayantara's cocked eyebrow—and left without asking their choices for the main course.

"We really should decide," Wayne said after meeting eyes with the waiter glancing at him over his shoulder.

"Some say sins are in the eyes of the beholder," Nayantara said.

She was at it again, boldly nudging him with her wit. He was obliged to engage and push back.

"Like beauty?" he said. "It's all relative?"

She smiled again. "That's a theory. But I think there's danger in it."

Wayne said, "Hell, I think there's danger in beauty. I've felt like I've been in danger from the moment I actually saw your face."

Nayantara cast her eyes downward as she lifted her glass for a sip. If she blushed, Wayne couldn't tell. Her body was speaking a language—something foreign—which he observed, recorded, and attempted unsuccessfully to decipher.

She met his eyes. "You said you were charitable. Too giving of yourself—right? If you're feeling at all threatened, maybe you've given yourself over to an ugliness. A bad seed. One you've mistaken for *beautiful*."

His picture of her was getting murkier, as ink dark as the Shiraz she sipped. Was this her feigned attempt at self-deprecation? It was a trait some men found attractive in women, but Nayantara couldn't pull it off. She was too beautiful and too accomplished for it to come off as sincere.

He had to step up his game, exploit this, and take her down.

"Oh, it's not just my eyes," he said, leaning forward. "I have a sixth, maybe even a seventh sense for these sorts of things. Things that are *truly* beautiful have a certain aura, one that can sometimes be seen but is more often inhaled, like the fragrance from the most exotic bouquet. The scent can be so delicate and yet so heavy that it finds its way through the nostrils and onto the tongue. Dear, I can see, smell, and *taste* true beauty."

"And not vomit?"

Wayne grimaced.

"Seems like the reasonable reaction," Nayantara said with a shrug. "Such an assault would surely make you dizzy at the least. And all those odors and tastes plodding on your buds . . ."

She'd knocked him on his rear. Mercifully, the waiter

returned to deliver their appetizers, giving him a chance to recover.

"We'll need about ten to decide on the main," Nayantara said.

The waiter nodded and slid away. Wayne's and Nayantara's eyes met before she lowered hers toward her soup. "Think this'll pair well with Shiraz, or should I order another glass?"

Wayne shook his head slowly. "I wouldn't know."

He was letting her overtake him. It couldn't be helped. By now, he should've been charming her, keeping her amused with anecdotes before launching into stories that would keep her enthralled as they feasted on the main course, all of it serving to weaken her while readying her for the truly sweet stuff to be delivered afterward. Instead, he was tongue-tied.

He closed his eyes and swallowed. He had to focus . . . focus on something she'd said, tie it up with a bit of his own high thinking, and gift it back to her.

"But . . . but I'm sure it will pair just fine," he said, "if the soup suits you as well as the wine does. It's said the best pairing is the wine you like with the food you like, regardless of rules about reds and whites, sauces and spices. The imbiber is the catalyst—the harmonizer. So long as she is beautiful, she can't go wrong with anything she ingests."

"Hmm." Nayantara tilted her head, nodded at him, then took her first spoonful of soup. The corners of her mouth twisted upward as she swallowed. The soup was good. She took a sip of Shiraz. Her eyes closed as her lips parted. "Oh . . ."

Yes, it certainly was a good pairing.

"Your palate thanks you," Wayne said.

"And *you*," she responded. "Perception is powerful, and it's not limited to the eyes. Sound, taste . . . Your words made this taste better than it should have."

He shrugged. "I don't know if I'm that talented."

"I'd bet against that. Your talents are probably even doing you in. In fact, I'd bet if you tasted the Shiraz now, you'd like it. Here." She pushed the glass toward him. "Have a few mushrooms first if you want."

He had a few fungi but stared warily at the glass. He didn't want that perfumed tar on his tongue again. And yet, there was a woman he still had to cultivate.

He sipped from the glass.

It was pure delight.

Nayantara nodded and smiled at him. "See? Nothing wrong with the wine, just the palate, which can be conditioned. It just takes a blind artist who knows how to work with unseeable materials."

"Ready to order?" Impatience evident in his voice, the waiter had returned. Wayne didn't want to keep the man on a string.

"Nayantara?"

She nodded. "I'll have the grape and walnut salad and a glass of the Pinot Blanc to help it down."

"And I'll have the salmon and a . . . umm . . ."

"Pinot Noir goes quite well with salmon." Nayantara passed him another sly smile. "Even without a psychological prompt."

"Then I'll have that," Wayne said.

The waiter nodded and left the table.

"You, uh . . ." Wayne chuckled. "You're all about the grapes tonight, huh?"

"Why not?" Nayantara said. "I'm out on a blind date. I don't know the man—*yet*—but I do know grapes; I liken their seeds to fragments of human souls. And souls need gathering, saving, *savoring* . . ."

Aw, great. Wayne winced as his scalp crawled. The game

they'd been kind of playing . . . the rules had changed at some point. He wasn't exactly sure when the woman had swerved him, but he knew where this was going.

"Wine can save the world," Nayantara continued. "Every enlightened woman and man, a viticulturist . . . What we do—what we produce—is based on the environment in which we live and work. We can work to produce something that will simply stain or that will elevate and inspire or, worst-case scenario, intoxicate and bring to ruin. The retributive Earth Goddess—"

Wayne stopped listening as he always did when it turned out his date was a nut. And Nayantara was the worst kind—a weirdo spiritualist nut. He should have known. Her beauty and background had been too good to be true.

He'd been here before. Hateful hippies, angry self-right-eous yogis, psycho vegans, smug Buddhists—he'd dated them all and had been invariably so turned off that he'd never pursued anything past dessert . . . when it had even gotten that far, which it usually hadn't.

It wasn't only his mind that was a master of interpretation; it was his total being. He could read body language, and his body had a reaction to language and its undertones. The reaction now was visceral. The crawling on his scalp spread over and penetrated his skin, then tickled and pricked his nerves until the mass of discomfort congregated in the area of his stomach. He was losing control of himself. Something was coming out.

"Excuse me." He hurried to the bathroom. Thankfully, it was empty—not that the presence of anyone else would've helped tamp down the sick that crawled up his throat. He managed to project all of it into a toilet bowl, but it took several heaves. He expelled a lot more than he'd taken in over the past day.

After he gave up all there was to give, he hefted himself up and shambled to the sink to rinse his face and throat. It was only when he finished drying that he checked the time on his phone. He'd been in the bathroom for close to an hour. That couldn't be right. But the sight of his table seemed to confirm.

Dinner had been served and mostly eaten. The woman's plate was clean. The food on his was cold. Her seat was empty. On his, she'd left an envelope, and inside were more than enough bills to cover the entire meal. There was also a folded note that had the word *tip* written on the outside. He unfolded it.

. . . so sweet, so sinful—decadence has a thin skin . . .

He shrugged off the nonsense and sat down to refill his stomach.

WAYNE ALMOST REGRETTED GETTING into bed. Something refused to let him alone.

It had started with his head rolling from cheek to cheek on his pillow, but it soon spread to the rest of his body. He tossed and turned, trying to find a position of even semi-comfort. It was a lost cause. He was just too damn hot.

It wasn't the mattress, the covers, or the room's temperature. It was something inside him—something in the pit of his stomach—as if he'd eaten a handful of Carolina Reapers before tucking himself in.

In a fit of frustration, he heaved the comforter and sheets onto the floor, then slipped off his pajamas, flinging them on top of the discarded bedclothes. The fire in his stomach remained, but being naked helped just enough.

He fell back in relief and sank, as if nestling into fresh, dry, *cool* sand. The memory foam mattress and pillow formed a mold for his body, cradling him as he fell into a deep, abiding sleep.

WAYNE FELT WARM, but it was a comforting warmth, like a tropical tide of pure bliss was slowly crawling in, touching him, teasing him, lapping at him, toying with him, clinging to him . . .

He'd wet the bed. And he was still wetting it.

Realizing, he tried to open his eyes, but it felt as if his eyelids had been glued shut. The glue was still wet and was drying fast. When he finally managed to part his lids, a heavy fog suffused with amber filled his vision. So concentrated, so *glutinous*, the fog stuck to his sight, preventing him from shutting his eyes.

Dreaming—he had to be.

He tried to turn to his side, but fatigue fought the effort. His movements were no different from those in a dream when some mugger, monster, or other vague villain was chasing him as he tried to escape. The foam mattress and pillow no longer felt like sand, not even wet sand. He didn't feel them at all. Over him, around him, under him—there was no bed, no furniture, no room. He was enveloped in some kind of aqueous gel.

He arranged and steadied his body like a wooden plank, stomach down, then let instinct take over. The environment wasn't right for walking or wading, so he jerked like a worm with limbs—languid appendages he wasn't yet sure how to use in a foreign environment. Soon, however, he felt less like a worm and more streamlined. His body was a more coherent whole, swimming the gel as he wondered a little about how he was actually breathing and a lot about where he was actually going.

Aimless for what seemed like an hour or more, he noticed a shimmering black dot. He swam toward it, thinking it might be an escape from all this. He swam faster and faster, straighter and straighter, watching the patch get bigger and bigger but no less mysterious, until he could go no farther.

He'd hit a curved barrier. Although firmer than the gel, the barrier was also pliable and transparent, or enough so for him to dimly see through, over the depths, across the expanse—his vision got sharper the more he gazed—through vales of varying shades of darkness until his sight hit its own barrier. He pressed himself closer to the membrane and concentrated, focused, letting his vision widen, adjust, as his head increasingly ached. It was approaching migraine territory when he made out a trace of a gargantuan, imperfect oval and got an inkling as to what was looking back, focusing on him.

I see that you're awake.

He heard the deep, feminine voice come from outside and within—all around—as he felt the gel quiver.

Shall I turn on the lights?

She did, and he trembled. The outline across the distance took on immediate color and definition, and the joyous smirking expression made it seem even more dimensional, almost overwhelmingly vivid.

The mirror image of Nayantara's face took up most of his view, but not so much that he couldn't tell that he was in a cramped bathroom—probably hers. She was illuminated only by a single bulb above the mirror, hardly what anyone would consider a vanity light; yet she seemed pretty pleased with what she was seeing: *him*, ensconced in her right eye socket, trapped inside her eye.

It seemed ludicrous to try to consider the physics or physiology of it all, but the questions involuntarily streaked through his mind: *Is she somehow seeing via me? Am I the lens of her eye? Part of the optic nerve? Am I somehow connected to her brain? What's inside her other eye? What else is inside this one?*

The flashing questions missed only the most obvious one, and it continued to elude him as she cracked another smile—wider, broader, *grimmer*—one so uncontainable it cracked the corners of her mouth, cracked the skin on her cheeks, her temples, across her nose, her forehead, all while her face steadily darkened to a deep reddish brown.

It was then that stark fear elicited the great question: "What are you?"

"Oh, sweetie," Nayantara said, "aren't you in the absolute perfect position to know?"

Greenish lines appeared in the fissures, lines that writhed and squiggled, attaining length and girth with each movement, becoming more like organic wires and sentient cords as they emerged, crawled, and spread over the increasingly uneven skin.

Wayne moaned. "I . . . don't know . . ."

"You will know," she said, "just what makes you *you.*"

In the mirror's image, Wayne saw the reverse of her right hand rush toward the eye before his view of everything pitched to nothing. The gel enveloping him shook slightly, then violently. His entire new world trembled and turned as he experienced a frisson and was tossed about, aimless, uncontrollable, witnessing flashes of golden light and blackness strike his minuscule planet until his body was pressed against the curved membrane, and his view was once again clear.

This time, he saw no reverse image. It was Nayantara's actual face transfigured—a region of untamed vegetation scarred by a grinning rocky gorge, all of it featuring one abnormally large piece of embedded fruit. There was a hole for another . . . or the seed of another. A temporary burial in the fresh wound from which fruit had just been plucked.

His sixth, seventh, or maybe even eighth sense kicked the realization into him.

"What makes a man but his hard labors?" he whispered as if induced by some gossamery angel. "What unmakes a man but the combination of his cracked actions?"

"*You? A man?*" Nayantara's laugh sounded like an avalanche in reverse. "You're just dessert."

She laughed once more before tossing him—his entire world—into the gorge.

Descending into the abyss, he grew less concerned about where he'd end up and more worried about the fragmented souls he'd be joining.

LOVE AMONG THE ULTRAMODERNS

The all-suite hotel promised the nicest lodging in Poagstown. He'd spent two hours doing the research before asking his secretary to book it. Even after a two-hour drive, most of it spent winding through poorly lit roads, he had a smile for the front-desk clerk.

The man gave a genuine smile in return before asking, "Name?"

"Rodgers."

The clerk handed him the key-card envelope before Rodgers even thought to give him a first name.

"I'll just need to see a credit card, Mr. Rodgers; then you can head on up."

Teresa had reserved the room using points, so he figured he might as well use the card that had earned them. He handed it to the clerk. "Where's the best place to get a bite at this hour? Someplace close."

"This hour?" The clerk eased his attention toward the clock sitting on the desk. "The steak house across the street closes in about forty-five. The bar next to it will be open later, but you probably don't want to put up with all that racket if you're tired. Otherwise, it's a hop, skip, and jump that way"—he hooked his thumb to the left—"to a few fast-food joints. That's about it." He handed back his credit card. "Welcome to our sleepy little family town, Mr. Rodgers."

Rodgers nodded, then headed toward the elevator. On the way up to the fifth floor, he chuckled. Poagstown was a way station, a town cluttered with little more than hotels, outlet shops, and a variety of eateries. The few people who actually lived here long term were probably related, or may as well have been.

And even though it was "sleepy" compared to DC, Poagstown wasn't so little—not as little as the town in which Bessa lived. That's why he'd chosen it. Small towns tended to be overpopulated with big-eyed, nosy sorts.

He walked into his suite. Teresa had done well. Tidy kitchen area, neatly arranged living room, and spotless bathroom. The queen-size bed he was expecting was closer to a king size. And the pulsating shower water was warmer than any he'd experienced during his other travels over the past four months. Best on-the-road shower this season.

After twenty minutes of scrubbing, he figured enough of Washington's stench had been washed away from his skin, and in the fifteen he spent getting dressed, he figured he'd accumulated enough northern-Maryland funk to wander into the dive bar across the street without pricking any busybody's senses. He wasn't exactly undercover, but his sub-missions did call for exercising a fair measure of discretion.

The joint seemed to cater mostly to hard-rock bangers and body-art aficionados, much as he'd expected. He had no tats, but he hoped his boots, jeans, and black leather jacket would make him seem less like an out-of-towner. Above the shoulders, he fit right in. He had the hair, he had the right look in his green eyes, and he could talk hard-core music—and hard-core anything else—with even the most intimidating chatterbox.

The bar had twenty stools but only eight warm bodies. He took a seat that gave him plenty of elbow room and a good enough view of the stage. The bartender looked in his direction. Even though the guy had never before set eyes on him, he nodded in a way that was more friendly than professional.

Rodgers let his shoulders slump, then gave his order. "Double IPA. Strongest one on tap."

The bartender nodded again, and Rodgers turned toward the stage. Two twentysomethings trying too hard with a retro-psychedelic look were trying even harder at playing and singing Hendrix. They divided duties and did well enough that Rodgers wasn't tempted to throw the glass of ice water the bartender had set in front of him, though he didn't know what the hell else to do with it. Water was for showering; his stomach was reserved for beer and maybe a burger. He wanted both his metaphorical and his actual guts ready for tomorrow's dirty deed—and this one, he had a feeling, would be damned dirty. He'd need that shower afterward.

He checked his smartphone. No new texts.

The bartender set a pint on the coaster in front of him. "Start a tab?"

"Uh, yeah, sure." He unthinkingly patted his jeans pockets for his wallet before finding it inside his jacket. He opened it, considered using the card that was racking up those ever-valuable travel points, but decided on using the generous gift card his secretary had given him for Boss's Day. He'd hopped on the horse of discretion; might as well ride it till he left town.

The bartender looked at the card, made the briefest eye contact with Rodgers, then glanced at the card again. "I'll be right back."

Rodgers sipped his IPA while keeping his eyes on the

bartender. Other than that momentary eye lock, the man wasn't acting suspiciously. Something bugged him, but, after taking a breath, Rodgers shrugged it off. Most likely the guy just wasn't used to folks paying with gift cards.

He sipped, then checked his phone again. No new messages. Bessa had promised to reach out by Wednesday afternoon. It was a little past nine. He hadn't heard from her since Tuesday morning. He hoped she hadn't left her phone where her husband could find it. Rodgers only knew her virtually, but he'd already figured her too daft to password protect anything.

"Here you go, Mister . . . ?" The bartender handed him his card.

"Johnson." Rodgers kept a wary eye on the man as he put the card back in its place.

"You been here before?"

"No—why?" He furrowed his brow.

"I was going to ask if you needed to see a menu, or if you already know what you want. Assuming you wanna chow?"

"Oh, yeah, sorry." He let his shoulders slump again. "I'll take a menu."

The bartender smiled and handed one over. "Name's Jet, by the way. Let me know if you need anything."

Rodgers nodded and scanned the menu. In the back of his mind, he knew what he had a taste for, and his eyes quickly found it. He motioned for Jet.

"Questions about the menu?"

"Only about how quickly you can get a Devil Burger out here." Half-pound burger with pepper jack cheese, fresh-cut jalapenos, three fried onion rings, and choice of sauce.

"How do you like it?"

"Medium rare. With the jumpin' jack sauce."

Jet nodded and went to punch it in. Rodgers tapped his

password into his phone. After being idle for more than ninety seconds, it had locked up. No new texts, so he scrolled up to the top of the chain he'd created with Bessa over the past week and reread it, prepping for tomorrow's body-and-mind 'scaping chores.

His message was first. He'd started the exchange after connecting with her on the Amorous Anonymous site and rapidly convincing her of his sincerity in helping with her body issues.

What time u want to meet on Thur?

Don't matter. Told huz I'm going to a friend's for the day. Time's unlimited.

Sounds good ;-) I'll probably drive up Wed night and get a room. So we can meet early for coffee if u want.

Drive up where?

Ur profile says you live near Borino . . . ?

Halfway between Borino and Poagstown. Borino is closer.

I'll get a room in Poagstown, is that okay?

Yeh. I get off at 8. After I shower, change, I can be there @ 9. Just want to have enough time for us.

Cum early ;-)

I will, if u don't ;-)

I can't wait—won't be able to stop thinking about u till then...

Hope u are more than a 2-min man. 10-min man?

I can go well over an hour ;-)

The back-and-forth went on for nearly a hundred more exchanges. In between the passing of smut and promises, Rodgers had picked up some details that weren't in the profile of the woman using the virtual name KissMeNewBe. The only information in her profile other than a blurry face pic was a summary of her age, height, weight, location, and status and two strings of words describing what she was looking for. She was north of fifty years old, about six feet tall, roughly two hundred pounds, a resident of the Wolfston, Maryland, area, and was—like almost everyone else on the site—"attached."

Through the various exchanges, Rodgers determined her real name—possibly—was Bessa. She was paid to work from 7:00 p.m. to 8:00 a.m. six days a week as a caregiver for the old and enfeebled. She wasn't paid or even appreciated for the care she gave to her husband, who'd fallen victim to some debilitating ailment shortly after their wedding ten years ago. In the wake of the tragedy, he became distant and even abusive toward her. Among all the other distorted perks of a relationship bound and twisted by the ties of illness and tradition, sex was absent. Love was a ghost. The words in her profile were simple: "Need someone to break my long dry spell. Been too long."

Rodgers had "favorited" her and sent her his private pic—the picture of his actual face to complement the picture of his well-defined pecs and abs on his public profile. He then sent her a message, introducing himself as "the Son of John," an unattached but job-holding man whose divine and devoted underground mission in life was to connect with women disappointed in their relationships in order to help them "find the sweet, soothing honey hidden in the dry valley."

Both verbally and physically, he put it different ways to different women, depending on each one's background, her personality, what he could glean about her situation, what she wanted, and what he felt she actually needed. Oftentimes, he had to resort to describing himself in so many words as a curious and hardworking itinerant immigrant, ever seeking out new lands where he might be of some use in helping rejuvenate what was worn out or overlooked and on the verge of being lost to the dust.

The message he'd initially used with Bessa was now lost to

the ether, thanks to the capacity limits of certain technologies, but whatever it was, it had gone over well with her. After a brief exchange of private emails via the site on Sunday, they began texting on Monday.

"Devil with pimpin' jack."

Rodgers's head jerked up. "*What?*"

"Devil Burg with jumpin' jack." The bartender set the sandwich and complimentary fries next to his near-empty pint. "Another beer?"

Lost in his thoughts, Rodgers had hardly been conscious of drinking it all this time. He nodded.

"Same?"

"Something a little stronger. That was good, but you got an IPA with a spicier kick to it?"

Jet laughed. "Hops ain't enough—the man wants *kicks* now. Got just the thing. Be back in a minute."

He was back in four with a clean glass and a new beer that had Rodgers smacking his tongue against the roof of his mouth. Perfect complement to the hot meal he'd begun.

"How's that burger?"

"Hits the spot," Rodgers said.

Jet nodded, then tended to a couple that had just sat down. Through vision more affected by alcohol than it should've been at that point, Rodgers focused on them. Something about the man and woman was familiar. He concentrated, tried to enforce an edge, will a *sharpness* to his vision—he had to be damn sure he didn't know them or, if he did, that they were fellow members of the club.

He was still drawing a blank when he heard his phone buzz. A text.

Hi Johnny... Johnny cum lately ;-) Have u made it UP yet?

He typed back. *Made it in about an hour ago. Finishing dinner now.*

Can't wait to c u. Been thinkin bout it all day.

Only a few hours to go.

2 many. u get to sleep. I have to watch over the graveyard.

:-) Morning will be here before u know it.

Where is ur hotel?

Don't know off the top of my head. I'll send the address when I get back to my room.

Can't wait to c it. And u. Tonite I used sum words I never used before.

He hesitated before responding. He scrolled back, scanning her texts, searching for anything unusual. Seeing nothing out of the ordinary, he typed back.

What do u mean?

Told my husband we were thru. Over now. I made him a quick simple dinner before I left. He wouldn't eat. Told him I was sleeping out. Left my ring on the table. He better not be there when I return. I called his brother to come get him. But enuff of my problems.

That was more than enough for Rodgers. That wasn't part of the plan. He wasn't sure what to type next, but Bessa had more to say.

If murder was legal, I think I'd have tried.

Rodgers moved his hands away from the phone as he gazed at the words.

Bessa sent another text.

Not really. But the idea. Shut him up. I can be a bitch when I want to be. Feeling better now.

This was going to be a challenge. He touched the screen to prevent it from locking. Bessa sent another message.

Do u still want to c me?

He had no choice—he'd taken an oath. And at this point on a sub-mission, only the sign of true mortal danger was an excuse for aborting, not just a bristling on the back of the neck.

Yes. Of course.

I'll wait for the address. Be careful heading back to ur room at this hour.

Rodgers turned his phone screen face down as Jet returned with a grin. "You sure loved that Black IPA. Want another one to wash down the rest of your meal?"

Rodgers looked at his empty glass. He must've downed it while lost in Bessa's words and the gnarly thoughts they'd inspired. He nodded to Jet, then continued to ponder what she'd said, getting hung up on one phrase: *If murder was legal.*

In what type of society—hell, in what type of *community*—would murder ever be legal? Would it even still be called "murder"? In Bessa's case, based on what little he knew, would it be considered justified? Bound to a man who couldn't please her and possibly wouldn't allow a divorce . . . The man was a burden, an abuser; he was practically keeping her in chains.

Rodgers and the other Errands hadn't wrestled with this before, not since he'd been a member. As far as he knew, there had never been a need. When it came to dealing with difficult spouses, the discussions usually focused on how to avoid them or deal with them if they came after you. The only philosophies they debated were the ones on which the Errands of Eros had been founded: those that centered on finding the bits and pieces of broken spouses and using methods to repair them— their relationships, too, if possible. Rodgers wasn't a violent man, even if his day job as an auditor required him to have a temper and get a little verbally rough every now and then. He wore his hair the way he did and tried to keep just a shadow of a beard in order to bump up the intimidation factor. But his demeanor, no matter which way it swung, was always for his clients' benefit, even if they didn't see it that way at first. They may have been in trouble and were getting into deeper trouble, but his job, ultimately, was to set them on the right track for the future. No different when it came to his after-hours social club.

Jet set a new glass in front of him. "So where you from?"

He forced a smile. He knew the bartender would try chatting him up sooner or later. Part of the job. Rodgers wasn't fully in the mood for a conversation, but he welcomed a distraction. "South of here."

"How long you in town for?"

"Two days."

Jet laughed. "That's about a day longer than most. You interviewin'?"

Rodgers shook his head.

Jet said, "I hear a coupla new outlet stores down the way have openings. Lot of people been coming through for that."

"Just passing through." Rodgers didn't want to continue on with clipped responses. Sooner or later, Jet was going to dig for what he was really in town for. He tried to divert him with more complete sentences. "But I don't like to pass through nice towns too quickly, know what I mean? There are some special ones where I like to take in the local color, let it color *me* a little, you know? So that I come out a different man."

"Yeah." Jet nodded. "Deep, man."

"I go as deep as I can when the mood strikes me."

"Well, if the mood strikes you tomorrow, you might want to check out the Dangerous Dimes bar, less than a mile away from here. Right now, you're drinking the best IPA we have on tap. But those fools over there? They got thirty different brews on draft, ten of them IPAs, half of them better than this one. Some weird, unique, crazy stuff."

Rodgers laughed. "Crazy, huh? Like you recommending another bar?"

"Hey, I just work here, man. My brother works over there. It's all good either way. You come back here if you want; I'll take good care of you. Go there for better care." He leaned in closer. "And you can bet the music's better. You'll get all the local color you can handle."

Rodgers nodded and asked to close his tab. Pleasure would have to come later. He needed a good night's rest for the landscaping he had to handle first.

He spent his last bit of energy during the walk back to his room checking over his shoulders.

<hr>

THE FIRE in his belly hadn't been a problem; it actually inspired some wondrously freaky dreams. It was the pounding in his temples that was slowing his morning pace. Still, he managed to get out of bed no more than fifteen minutes after his wake-up call. He showered and was indulging in the free continental breakfast by eight. He made it quick, downing as much fruit, toast, and coffee as he could in half an hour. He needed time to brush his teeth and stretch out before Bessa arrived.

He was dozing at 9:17 when his phone buzzed. A text.

Just pulled in.

Bessa. He texted his room number to her and told her to come on up.

OK ;-)

The moment of truth. How accurately had she portrayed herself in her profile? He'd expected some disconnect; they all fudged a little. Didn't matter though, just so long as she wasn't really a man.

There was a knock at the door. He checked the peephole.

Yeah . . . He could see how that face, made slightly indistinct, could match the woman's profile. He cracked the door.

"Bessa?"

She smiled, revealing only five teeth he could see—all of them shading between yellow and green and each separated by generous space.

He opened the door all the way and invited her in. She was certainly eye level with him—five foot eleven—but it looked like she'd underreported her weight by at least fifty pounds. Even though she may've showered, she was wearing what she'd probably worn on her graveyard shift—a beige jumper dress with a faded floral print on the arms and collar and a slightly orangish stain to the left of the stomach area. It wasn't recent; the dress had probably gone through more than one wash cycle since the tomato-soup or whatever-the-hell incident, but considering the size of the residue and the size of her stomach, it was hard to miss.

She set her purse on the kitchen table and, smiling again, turned her eyes to his. He forced a smile, then allowed it to relax into one more comforting.

"Please"—he gestured toward the couch—"have a seat. Let's talk."

She was hesitant but complied. Rodgers sat on her right, leaving a foot of space between them.

"So," he said, "tell me a story."

She gaped at him.

"I mean, tell me your issues with your man. How did you leave it with him?"

"Lance?" She guffawed. "That's over. Left the ring on the sink. His brother's there now takin' care of him. He can feed him. Wash him. When I go back, if I go back, I'm kickin' his ass out."

Her accent was as rural as he'd expected. Southwestern Pennsylvania in origin, best he could judge. Not a college graduate. Not even an applicant. Community college was a possibility, but he wouldn't take those odds. He'd played down his true background while they were messaging and thought it best to continue that way as he took care of the chores.

"You have really pretty eyes," he said honestly. "Maybe, with what happened to him, he hasn't been able to look at them in all these years—*really* look at them—and remember why he fell in love with you. You shouldn't just—"

"Fuck 'im. He didn't fall in love with me because of my damn eyes. I chased 'im. He had a good job, and my first husband left me with shit. But Lance, he begun cheatin' on me before the honeymoon. Psycho . . . Nothing I could do about it. The sclerosis stopped it though, boy, right quick. I stayed 'cause I felt obligated. He made me feel like I had to."

Rodgers switched to level two. If there was no hope of convincing the damaged spouse that love might still exist with her mate, then—"He needs you, and you just need some on the side. You're in the right place."

"He used to be somebody, you know. A good mind. That's why I married him. Really knew how to cook. *Really* cook. Make recipes. Had good ideas."

She was too frazzled for anything Rodgers had to say to do any good. Best to save it for pillow talk. He inched closer, put his arm around her shoulders. "*I* have ideas." He moved his face closer to hers. Her lips seemed to lunge for his. He fought his instinct to flinch. They locked.

The first kiss began about an hour's worth of foreplay. It was well into hour two when Rodgers fully undressed her and allowed her to undress him. After ensuring he was well protected, he put her through every sexual position he could manage, guiding and instructing Bessa the entire way. Even though she was fifteen years his senior, she had the sexual experience of a fourteen-year-old.

It wasn't the first time he had made love to someone who outweighed him by at least a hundred, but it was a perpetual challenge, a fierce workout. His four years of high school wrestling came in handy.

More than three and a half hours after their first kiss, they finally rested in each other's arms, lying on the bed that had helped host his bizarre dreams just a few hours before. Bessa was on the verge of sleep. Rodgers, despite having spent himself, was more awake than ever.

At some point during the experience, he agreed to let her spend the night. He didn't want her to go back home; he wasn't sure of her state of mind. She couldn't afford a room of her own. And he wasn't callous enough to let her sleep in her car as she suggested, no matter how many times she claimed to have done it before.

Hell, he had no choice. He was an auditor, a would-be saint, an encourager of closed women. A prier. A *freer*. He opened those who were willing to open themselves, then he steered them, guided them, setting them on the right course. His will freed theirs.

He was one among the many Errands of Eros, who were originally the Errant Knights of Eros until they began inducting female members. The revised name had come from the idea that, as an "Errand," they were the object of a short trip (sometimes many) taken by a troubled spouse to cure what ailed them.

They were a chivalrous group, seeking out sexually starved wives—and, more recently, husbands—and doing whatever could be done to satiate them. The way to a famished person's brain is her or his stomach, real or metaphorical. The heart thing was dangerously misleading. Hearts were nothing but pulsing tangles of muscle, blood, and nerves—a confusion of passion, lust, and hate. *Murderous* . . . The head was the region from which love actually sprang—true love—forgiveness, mercy, and all that was related. The brain was where the action was. The ever-mysterious brain—ever attempting to contain the roiling seas of the conscious and subconscious—was nursed and sustained by the stomach, not the heart.

Rodgers and his fellow Errands tried to help the unsated rediscover the love they had for their significant others or, barring that, rediscover the benefits of the relationship. When there were few benefits to be found, the Errand would encourage the exploration of an open marriage or polyamory. But when that failed, the Errand would secretly meet with the wandering spouse every so often to fill his or her sexual needs— Option Four. It was the least desirable of options, but it was always on the table. The only thing that wasn't on the table was divorce. Divorce could be a hell of a lot worse than a marriage of convenience, and not only for any kids that may have been involved. The Errands took an oath and worked hard to prevent The Big D at all costs.

But Rodgers wasn't sure where he stood with Bessa. Her state of mind didn't seem to improve any during sex. He needed to feed her, talk to her more, ensure she was facing the right direction.

He pushed his attention toward her, ready to cushion her thoughts with pillow talk. Her snoring made him think a bull was about to come through the room.

He nudged her—harder when the first didn't work. She didn't stir until the point when it seemed he was rousing a bear from hibernation. "Huh?"

"Uh, want to grab a bite?"

"Mm . . . if you want."

"Like steak?"

Yes, she did. But, at the steak house, she ordered only a quarter of the amount of food he did. Ravenous, he got the biggest rib eye on the menu. It was just as well. She was more interested in talking than eating. Even though Rodgers ate as quickly as he could, he listened—politely—to the longest tale of woe he'd ever heard, a tale winding through parents, boyfriends, and husbands and the various abuses they'd visited upon her. She'd gotten her licks in as well, but the experiences —Rodgers surmised more than he heard her say outright— resulted in psychological damage, wildly fluctuating body weight, and a host of other issues that made her feel as unattractive inside as she felt on the outside. The words *dog* and *cow* and their various synonyms came up frequently. Rodgers had no appetite for dessert.

It was a slow trod back to the room. The two exchanged weak but playful banter, hinting with trepidation about round two of sex, which could only occur after their food had settled.

Bessa heaved herself down onto the couch and picked up the TV remote.

"I'll be in the bathroom. Excuse me a minute." He was in there for more than fifteen, attempting to relieve his bowels while he focused on his smartphone, checking his messages, responding to a few, and scouring the AA site for near-future missions. The rounds completed, he turned his thoughts to Bessa. He'd have to choose Option Four. But where would she stay in the meantime?

He wiped, flushed, and washed. They'd have to talk it out, and he wouldn't get back in bed until there was a resolution.

Bessa was standing near the kitchen table when he came out, purse slung over her shoulder. "I have to go."

"Wh—? Why?"

"The . . . there's been an accident. I can't stay."

"Oh." He didn't quite understand but didn't want to press for details. "Well, when can I see you again?" They'd need a set schedule in order for Option Four to work.

"I'll send you a text." She turned for the door. "It's been wonderful, John. I hope to see you again."

She opened the door and was through it before he could play the gentleman. She'd thrown him a curve. But if and when she sent him the text, he'd get it all straightened again.

JET HAD BEEN RIGHT about the music at Dangerous Dimes. The portly, bald, and bearded man on stage was like a one-man death-metal band. Deep voice thrown and complex riffs played—sometimes above his head or behind his back—all while sitting on a wobbly stool in front of a microphone. He had the people dancing. Even the roughnecks playing pool on the opposite side of the room were banging their heads.

Rodgers had been drinking brews for an hour before deciding to order a burger with the spiciest ingredients.

"It'll pass through you," the bartender had said when setting it in front of him, "but not too quickly. Know what I mean?"

The only thing Rodgers knew was it was one of the best burgers he'd ever tasted, though it did no favors for his digestive system. Well, hell, he'd take some antacid after he got back to his room.

His phone vibrated in his pocket. A text—but it wasn't from Bessa. It was from his secretary.

Have the accommodations been satisfactory?

Teresa had never texted him before, at least not unprompted, and certainly not on his club-issue phone. He'd given her the number and instructed her to use it only in an emergency.

Wonderful, he responded.

Have you been eating well?

Yeah. I'll see and tell you all about it soon.

:-)

He placed his phone back in his pocket and shook his head. It was a Friday night. Maybe she'd gone out with some of the girls and had had a little too much to drink. He decided to be lenient and not to bring it up when he saw her on Monday, not unless she did.

A woman took the empty stool next to him. He glanced, then did a double take when he realized she looked vaguely familiar. Before he could place her, she smiled, and he reactively smiled back, keeping it friendly. The woman was a looker, but he'd no intent to seduce. He'd had more than enough for one weekend.

"Ever been lovesick?" she asked.

His smile wavered. "Uh . . . you mean like missing a girl?"

She shook her head. "Like working so hard to make love work, willing so hard to make what you think is 'love' work, that you end up making yourself sick."

Barstool philosopher. In his experience, they were usually men, and he usually humored them. He wasn't in the mood, but he didn't want to be rude.

He shrugged—"Maybe"—then reached for his beer. "I've been sick after making love—does that count?"

The woman grinned while he sipped. "I only asked because you look a little pale, and my intuition is telling me it has something to do with a woman."

He wasn't sure what she was getting at, so he thought he'd go a little bolder. "That's an odd pick-up line."

She grinned again. "I'm not trying to pick you up. I'm just concerned about my customers."

He cocked his head.

"I'm part owner of the bar."

He looked at her the same way he'd looked at her the night before, but with a bit more clarity. She was the woman he'd seen at Jet's bar. But she was without her partner.

"I noticed you seem to be enjoying the food and beer more than the other attractions in here. Would you like to take a peek behind the scenes, get an idea of how we prepare everything?"

"Uh, sure. Why not?" He rose as she did.

"Don't worry," she said. "The bartender will make sure no one messes with your stuff."

He followed her, trying his best to figure where he'd seen the woman prior to Thursday night. The disturbance in his stomach must have been messing with his memory. Overall, he hadn't been at his best the past couple of days, and as they continued down the hall, he was almost prepared to write off the whole excursion as a failure. Mission unaccomplished— depending on whether he ever saw or heard from Bessa again.

The hallway seemed to become more winding, the floor more uneven, the lights dimmer.

"Is, uh, the kitchen all the way back here? I think we've come a long way from the bar."

"No," the woman said. "This is where we process the spices. The sort of ingredients that guys like you love so much."

"Guys like—?" He lost the rest of his words when they turned into a well-lit room.

He now recognized the woman and her partner. Seeing the three of them together, he remembered that both of them had been at his secretary's wedding. Teresa's brother and sister. And they now stood in a row—shoulder to shoulder—brother and sister on either side of their sibling. Reminiscent of how they did years ago, in the wedding that took place in this area. Two years before the divorce.

"Evening, boss."

"Teresa? What are you doing here?"

"My job."

The room had rows upon rows of shelves full of boxes and

bottles, each labeled in code. A variety of secret ingredients, perhaps, for a variety of potential concoctions.

Teresa beckoned him with a finger and began down a row. Her brother and sister stepped aside to let him follow her down the row and into a broader aisle that ended in a wide, open area.

A hoary, frail, wheelchair-bound man sat in the middle of the clear space and glared at him. Behind the man stood another, his hands grasping the wheelchair's handles. Several feet behind them, an open door the size of a barn's gave view to the nighttime open air and a parking lot, filled now with just a couple of trucks. They were in a supply receiving area.

His eyes fell again upon the glaring man's, and a different sensation struck his bowels—dozens of tiny eruptions, minute explosions of gas and what seemed like glass.

"So," the old man rasped, "how was my wife?"

Of course, Rodgers thought. *Lance.*

"Was she good?"

"Listen," Rodgers said, "I—" He tried to push forward a coherent explanation, one of the short-and-sweet speeches all Errands were required to memorize and regurgitate in such code-red situations, the equivalent of a tortured soldier's name, rank, and serial number, but he merely lapsed into incoherent stuttering, his shifting bowels and throbbing stomach doing him no favors.

As Teresa approached the wheelchair, Rodgers's eyes focused on her. He completely forgot all his memorized language. All he could manage was "Teresa . . . What is this?"

She shook her head. "Oh, boss, boss, boss . . . Who else but me would know everything about you? Your taste in accommodations, your taste in libations, your taste in food, your *sick* taste in women . . ."

The man behind the wheelchair—Lance's brother, no

doubt—released his grip and walked toward the wide-open door leading to the lot. Teresa took his place.

"Knowing where you were rooming and the hour you'd arrive, it was easy to guess which bar you'd probably go to. I made sure to let my cousin Jet know—and my other cousins. I told them to give you the family welcome, to make sure you were well fed, to ensure everything you ate gave you a little kick inside, pushing you in the right direction."

As she mentioned it, his insides felt as if his abdomen's organs were turning to dust, his blood to vinegar . . . Not dust, more like baking soda . . . the reaction between it and his poisoned blood resulting in more and more furious fizzing. He wanted to vomit—he wanted to *shit*—but nothing was going anywhere. Nothing inside him made any movement to exit. He doubled over, arms crossed, hands clutching his sides. Through the panting and wheezing, he managed a guttural "*Why?*"

Jet walked in from the parking lot. An ax rested on his shoulder. "When two clubs square off," he said, "how else is one to overcome without predicting or even guiding the opponent's every move?"

"Clubs?"

"The Errands of Eros being just one," Teresa said.

"You have your oath," her sister said, "and we have ours."

"To gather and cull those who step beyond acceptable boundaries while seeking to solve Love's mysteries."

"Your club isn't alone," Teresa said, "but it will soon be gone, as will the others."

Rodgers screamed as something long and sharp—*two* somethings—plunged into his back, above his kidneys. It was the brother and sister; they'd stuck him with something he imagined as javelins . . . spears . . . or long arrows. Whatever they were, the wielders lifted them in conjunction, like a meat-turning fork, forcing the doubled-over Rodgers to stand erect.

They apparently wanted him to have a good view—as good as his bleary eyes would allow—of Lance's brother reentering the room, pulling the harness of what at first appeared to be a severely deformed farm animal, one with the size of a bull, the stance and awkward gait of a morbidly overweight bulldog, and the pale-white hide of a polar bear randomly interrupted with blue-purplish splotches. It seemed to be foaming at the mouth.

Through his groaning, sobbing, and gnashing, Rodgers heard old man Lance. "Bessa and I had a good ol' talk today. Better'n the one we had yesterday. Yesterday, she wanted to leave me. But she had to be reminded she took a sacred oath. She told me you didn't quite satisfy her. I sure as hell wasn't satisfied. I listened patiently, heard where she was coming from, and I decided to allow her another chance. This time, on my usual terms."

Rodgers saw the man's deranged grin and again met his eyes. Bessa had been right. Her husband was an absolute monster, a *psycho*, but not in the way he'd originally imagined. Lance could do little with his body other than use his eyes to suck and his mind to feed off his wife's pleasures. That's how he dreamed up recipes. That's how he made creations that were out of this world.

Rodgers didn't have to surmise—he *knew* it all. When his and Lance's eyes locked, they experienced stuttered moments of symbiosis. *Psycho . . . pair of psychos . . . parapsycho . . .* And now, his eyes and the creature's were nearly locked, the two of them less than a dozen feet from one another. The familiar eyes . . . Yesterday, they'd been much closer.

"*My* terms," Lance said. "I pick the partners. Out-of-town-ers. After the deed is done, in their sleep, I work my culinary magic."

His brother undid the harness. Jet came up from behind

the creature, passed on its left side. Rodgers's stomach felt ready to burst; his insides were a raging churn.

Jet stood in front of him, between him and the metamorphosed Bessa. "Things got a little out of whack this time around." He reached for Rodgers's collar and ripped open his shirt. "But we'll set it straight."

Jet used the ax to punctuate his promise. Rodgers screamed as the blade tore into his abdomen and again as it tore into his side, just under his ribs. After another whack, the siblings behind him let go of their utensils. He was free to fall on the floor, writhing, hollering, bellowing, dimly watching the mushy meal—the remains of the ground beef and beer he'd consumed mixed with his own blood and putrefied innards—ooze onto the floor. Bessa made a deep-sourced lowing sound. Most of the extended family laughed.

"These good ol' family recipes get 'er goin' every time!"

"Recognizes the cycle of life, man."

"Yeah, we got this one cooked and tenderized just the way she likes."

Bessa dipped her head down and lapped up the ooze. Rodgers's consciousness wafted away to some imperceptible realm. He was far from being able to process the last twenty-four hours, let alone the last twenty-four minutes. He could only attempt the last several seconds.

She was now just a beast; she may've always been just so. He was now just a meal; he may've always been just so. Or maybe, intermittently in life, he was she, and she was he . . .

Teresa stood at his head. "We strive to keep relationships fresh." She grinned at something he was too far gone to comprehend.

He gurgled. "You . . ." Bessa gnawed on his orange-pinkish flesh.

"*We* merry feasters, we sippers of Eros, we Culinaries of

Cupid—we savor the good bits and pieces of broken fool lovers and serve the waste to others of their kind."

His eyes closed and did not reopen. He could no longer breathe. Words came to him like grains of sand down an ever-tightening funnel.

"Another one of your fraternity is flying here in a few days. By then, Bessa will have digested you. I thank you in advance, boss, for providing us with the ingredients we'll need to help your brother feel right at home."

THE LURE

"Don't let a Great One get away . . ."

The once-whispered words lingered in Aoife's mind like sea mist, evaporating only when present awareness crept in. She opened her eyes. Her head rested on her right arm, outstretched, cold and flat against the desk. Her hot-pink tablet, in power saver mode, was inches in front of her nose. She was still in the chair—and the man had long gone. But his scent remained—hints of green mandarin and ginger from his cologne with stronger notes of mildew. It seemed she just wouldn't rid herself of Fergus so easily.

He'd only passed through the room twice, an extended round trip from her cabin's door to the balcony. Odd that he should leave such a fusty mark. Though his intentions (she thought) were clear, it was even odder that not once in his short travels had he even glanced at the bed—unlike Aoife. Dry bubbly and drier conversation on the verandah had been enough to send her napping after she'd dismissed her latest would-be suitor. But she'd never made it to her pillows. She'd fallen asleep while filling her journal with her latest findings.

Now, she felt dehydrated—cotton mouth and all. That called for a quick fix. Hydration, after all, was a large part of how her magic worked.

She downed a quart of water, then stripped off her tropical sundress as she made her way to the bathroom, tossing it on the tightly made bed and sliding off her flip-flops just outside the bathroom door.

Magic . . . She couldn't help but grin, chuckle aloud at the thought followed by the sight in the mirror. Skin too pale, eyes too big, nose too hooked, and smile too crooked. She saw it every morning—had been seeing it for three decades. Age only emphasized the unpleasant features while sneakily adding a few new ones. Age spots competing with the freckles she'd endured since youth, gray-streaked auburn hair ever more resistant to fashionable styling, and extra padding in areas that made parts of her look like unbaked dough. She could count each imperfection that should have warded men off and often did count them while showering. Presently, she did so with a smile on her face, rubbing herself down with her own special blend of bodywash. While the creamy gel permeated her skin, the resulting fragrance would clear out the stubborn remnants of Fergus.

She left her sweet-smelling cabin dressed in an ash-green sleeveless jumpsuit, a wide-brimmed straw hat, and sandals. Thank heavens the day-and-night dress code was "resort casual." She'd made no attempts during her journey on the high seas to look her best. That was part of the test—to see if her charms would really work. She did have limits to how low she'd go, however. After scratching herself and drawing blood twice while trying to comb her hair, she couldn't hold off getting her nails done any longer.

The sky was clear, aqua colored. Aoife took a deep breath, enjoying the sea smells, then stumbled. She dropped her bag but caught herself, instinctually examining the floor, ready to assign blame even though she knew it was her usual two left feet. There were no objects lying out of place, but there was something off about the wood flooring. Here and there among the normal brown were off-color patches; hand-size geometrical patterns reminiscent of mollusk shells. They were few and far between, but as she walked on, she noticed similar patches on the walls. She brushed her fingers against one as she passed. Texture, temperature—it felt no different from the nonpatched areas. Probably just an effect of the light in the sky. Or maybe being who-knew-where-exactly in the Atlantic with nothing else around was finally getting to her, playing tricks on her, just as she, the incongruous beauty, had been playing tricks, focusing the bulk of her attention on the men. They happily reciprocated, as now, passing her in their golf shirts and shorts, a variety of hats and sunglasses, and wide toothy smiles.

Ah, the merry men . . . All unmarried (allegedly) and ranging from handsome to gorgeous. The women on board covered a much wider spectrum. Aoife didn't even consider herself in the middle of the range. Others saw her much differently.

"*Look* at her . . . the dirty *witch* . . ."

Two women in white cropped pants passed her with twin outfits, sour expressions, and deleterious mutterings. Aoife tried not to shudder, tried to pass without showing she'd heard, noticed, or cared. But all the soul-sipping whispers, the withering looks . . . She'd gotten them from day one. On day three, they were more obvious, vicious, and spirit draining. She felt a layer of moisture forming on her forehead. Her palms were too warm, her armpits sticky. All these *heated* women—they were a threat. She couldn't allow herself to sweat out of fear or embarrassment. "*Perspiration does not inspire,*" Cyrena had warned.

She lowered her eyelids as she continued to walk the

boards, maintaining just enough attention not to bump into anything while mostly concentrating on her heart, stilling it, controlling her breathing. She even caught hints of her odoriferous aura and, inspired, added self-visualization to her method . . .

She was an exotic flower, emitting scents redolent of a paradise known only through genetic memory, not actual experience. As she moved fearlessly through the world, she exuded a sweet scent tempered by hints of melancholy, turning heads, making her seem irresistible, truly beautiful, while implying a hint of vulnerability. She didn't want to seem too unattainable; heck, she *wanted* to be attained eventually—gathered up and absorbed by a truly desirous lover—but she didn't want to seem too easy either. She wanted men who not only detected the hints of sadness but would genuinely want to do whatever they could to erase them. That was how she and Cyrena had formulated the concoction. Fear rendered it noxious, toxic. But the fruits and herbs, flowers and oils, animal excretions and man-made chemicals, all working together as they should, propelled by the right attitude? *Magic* . . . And she would use it, all the way to the island and back.

By the time she entered the salon, she was as cool and tranquil as the distant waters seemed. It was her second visit since yesterday's massage, and she was still amazed; she'd never heard of a beauty salon staffed entirely by men—not that she was complaining. She took an empty seat in front of a fair-haired man who offered, among other services, a hot oil manicure. The young man smiled as he met her eyes and gently took her hands, caressing her fingers even before he placed them in the bowl to wash them. "How are you today, Ms. Finnegan?"

"Umm . . ." She studied his tanned, boyish face but couldn't place him. "I'm good." How did he know her name? He looked at her as if she should know his.

"Meyers, ma'am." He smiled, perhaps at the unfortunate alliteration. But there was also a hint of something behind his gray eyes and at the corners of his mouth. "I am happy you're enjoying yourself."

"Yes." Aoife grinned awkwardly. "Well, to be completely honest, I just woke up from a nap, but don't think I'm all there yet. Maybe I need some coffee."

"Maybe. But you know, coffee saps you more than it fills you."

She grinned again, no less awkwardly. "Maybe you're right. But I don't know; I've been feeling a little off since breakfast."

"Or maybe you're just feeling *it*."

She cocked her head.

"The closer we get to La Isla, the more people around here feel it. Come into their own, you know?" He winked at her as he dried her hands. Aoife's brows drew closer.

La Isla del Amor. A remote island in the Atlantic. A fantasy island. All kinds of luxury cruises had sailed for it. Not one had found it. A few too many had ended in tragedy. For liability reasons, most companies had long ago redirected their routes, taking their tours to more well-known islands, populated islands, destinations more stable if not more fabled. Only one line still made the attempt—a venture both romantic and heroic—and all such trips, appropriately, were for singles only. The island was off the charts, both literally and in levels of exoticism, rumored to appear only periodically to the worthy, a ship of lovesick fools. Allegedly, it was roughly a four-day trip from port. If the island didn't emerge for all to experience, the cruise would spend another four days heading back. It was a silly legend to be sure, but the journey was supposed to be a fun adventure. And it had been, until today. Aoife didn't feel like she was coming into anything, only perpetually dipping and diving.

Meyers briefly caressed her left hand before he began to file. "Mr. Palm Reader," she said. "What do you think it means that I can't keep my eyes open?"

His glistening eyes stole a glance at her drier ones. "Dreams. Important ones. About destiny."

"Oh? Could you possibly tell me what I've been dreaming about? Because I'm not remembering much of anything."

"Well, you know . . ." He shrugged. "When you sail for parts unknown to man . . . or mostly unknown."

"You've actually seen the island?" she asked, only half-incredulous. "Been there?"

He shook his head. "But those of us who work here, we've seen signs. We've come close."

"Yeah." A harsh voice spoke up from her right. "Many of us feel the same."

Aoife turned to see a hefty woman receiving a pedicure two chairs down. Meeting Aoife's eyes, she clicked her teeth at her. "Looks like Miss Thang has already been into her own, as well as into some of what the rest of us should be owning."

Jean, she thought the malcontent's name was. They'd met on the first night, frostily. Their relationship hadn't warmed any since then, with Jean eyeing the same men who eyed Aoife most intensely.

"Ma'am," Meyers said to her, "please. If you don't mind—"

"Oh, look!" Jean raised her voice. "The first attention any halfway-decent-lookin' man has paid me since I've been on this ship, and he's tellin' me to shut up!"

"Uh, Jean, right?" Aoife said. "I have no qualms with you. We are all here for a good time, right?"

Jean clicked her teeth again. "Listen, missy, you're the only one makin' out good. You need to start savin' some for the rest of us."

"Excuse me, I don't see how what I'm doing or not doing is any of your concern."

"Oh?" Jean chuckled without humor as she slipped on her sandals and stood, reaching into her handbag. "You'll see, girly." She tossed some bills in the direction of the pedicurist and stormed off.

"Sorry about that." Jean's pedicurist spoke in a near monotone as he gathered up the ones and fives.

"Yes," Meyers said. "Our guests shouldn't harass other guests. It's usually the opposite sex in conflict."

"I'll make the call." The pedicurist picked up the phone on his desk and muttered into it.

Aoife sighed. The woman had made a point, one others had heretofore only whispered about. Yeah, she was doing well with the men, but she wasn't having all the luck. She'd seen her share of hand-holding, kissing, and caressing that in no way involved her. But it was equally true her presence within a certain proximity did crush up others' affections, evoking smiles from the men, less pleasant expressions from the women.

She needed a drink. She shut her eyes as big men in nice blazers, responding to the pedicurist's call, surrounded her—ostensibly to protect her from other attacks. When Meyers dipped her hands into warm oil, she fought hard not to doze.

MEYERS WOKE her by gently tapping her wrists. After opening her eyes with a jolt, Aoife smoothed over her embarrassment with a crooked grin. "Umm, how much, please?" She reached for her handbag.

Meyers held up his hand. "Gratis, Ms. Finnegan. We're sorry you were harassed."

"Oh . . . But a tip at least—"

He winced, shaking his head, then met her eyes with a smile. "Just have a drink with me later."

She smiled back. She needed one now.

After nodding her goodbyes to Meyers and the leering guards who'd ensured her safety, she made her way unsteadily toward the club at the back of the ship with the outdoor buffet. It was late afternoon—too early for dinner. But they served from sunup to late in the evening. They'd take care of her, or so she hoped.

Her body felt increasingly strange—tight skin, loose muscles working against each other, and flimsy thoughts. Light-headed, she wondered what'd happened while she was asleep, then her eyes fell on the patches. They were bigger now, the size of torsos, and all the more prominent as their colors seemed faintly luminescent. The patterns were beautiful, definitely like seashells; she couldn't help but run her fingers over a patch on a wall as she passed. They had a strange texture, like flecks of cracked, peeling paint. She withdrew her fingers and examined the tips. Nothing had rubbed off, but she thought it best not to tempt fate further.

The club was a blur of activity. The first thing Aoife could focus on were cobalt-blue eyes . . . Gareth's smiling face. "I trust you'll do me the pleasure of gracing my meek presence?" Cute, sweet, and entertaining. She'd met him on day one, had taken to him on day two. On day three, he was still her favorite. He tried to speak like a character from a mid-twentieth-century romance movie, but it always came out sounding off-kilter and weird—endearing but funny. She liked men who made her laugh. He would cure whatever was ailing her.

She tried to match him. "I will join you at your table if you bring me a bounty to keep me buoyant. I need a pick-me-up, but I can't exactly pick my own up."

He gave her a funny look before she held up her hands,

palms down, and wriggled her shiny nails. He smiled, nodded, and guided her around whispering and muttering bodies to the table he'd occupied before she arrived. He then drifted away toward the buffet. Focused on his well-tailored sports jacket, Aoife's eyes followed him till they seemed to drift on their own accord toward the other men near her, gazing at her. None made a move or even spoke a word. They'd seen she'd made her choice for the hour, so they kept their distance, respectfully. Still, they couldn't help but leer. She tried not to entice; at this point, though, she didn't know how. Feeling the creep of embarrassment, she trained her gaze on the tabletop—a soothing hue of green.

"Men are just stomachs."

The frazzled voice unsettled her tranquil thoughts. It had come from the table to her left. Aoife didn't turn her head but couldn't help but give it her full attention.

"They only want to feed their appetites. They're lust machines. They don't think rationally. They just adjust their worldviews to fit their desires. And those rag dolls—those so-called women who let themselves be used—they accept that view while the rest of us are pushed to the side, the shadows, to *wither* and *die*."

The speaker uttered those last words with such malice, Aoife couldn't help but open her eyes and peek at her. She didn't recognize her, but one of her three companions—Jean—was all too familiar. All four seemed to be competing on who could glare the hardest.

Aoife's eyes immediately went back to the soothing green tabletop. The women were just bitter. They had found themselves on a love boat where they weren't even wanted, let alone needed. They weren't close to finding love, so they waxed philosophical over cocktails too hot for umbrellas. Aoife couldn't help but feel pity, even as she realized such a feeling was condescending.

"Oh, you got a *problem*, Miss Thang?" Another woman from the same table spoke up.

Aoife sighed. Evidently, "Miss Thang" was her nickname among the ladies who'd criticized her behind her back and now —coming into their own—to her face. She turned partway in their direction. "No. No problem, girls. We're all in this together, you know?"

"Oh yeah," Jean said, "you're all in. For *yourself. Girl.*"

Aoife turned back, resuming her table-ward gaze. *Bunch of harpies.* There was no reasoning with them, no making friends. This was becoming less of a pleasure cruise and more of a back-stabbing convention—a seminar for cutthroats. Heck, it may as well have been the day job, where everyone jockeyed for posi-tion, for attention, for reward, while those left behind or below sharpened their knives and plotted.

She grabbed her bag and left the table, almost stumbling twice, as she made for the buffet area. She wanted to find Gareth and tell him, "Another time." Halfway there, she saw him emerge from behind a large plant in front of her, holding two plates. One, laden with crustaceans and asparagus, he extended to her. "A paradisiacal feast for you." He nodded at the other with a sheepish grin. "Sometimes a man just feels like a fish sandwich."

She was too flustered to even pretend to laugh. "See you later, 'kay?"

His brows knit together. "Where are you going?"

"To get some fresher air."

"But—"

She dashed in the direction of the nearest washrooms, losing her hat without a worry. A moment before entering the ladies' room—a sure hotbed of dirty looks and dirtier whispers —she cut right, entering an unmarked door on a whim.

It was a room for cleaning supplies. She sighed relief. Here, she could truly be alone. She leaned against a shelf that held containers of liquids and powders, all created to sanitize but that, when used improperly or with malice, could easily wash a life into oblivion. She laughed and kept laughing to stave off an impending anxiety attack. It took a force of will to stop herself from tripping over the edge into pure hysterics. To think that working in a lab all day surrounded by women who complained incessantly about their husbands had brought her *here*.

Really it was all Cyrena's fault. The violet-eyed brunette with the long legs and the perfect cheekbones had insisted that Aoife's bad luck with men had little if nothing to do with looks, far more to do with attitude. And a healthy attitude feasted on confidence. Substance was all the style she needed. If she wanted to receive love, she had to open herself to it. That was all easy for Cyrena to say; she really hadn't known Aoife that long.

The brunette had originally worked for a competing cosmetics lab before Aoife's lab hired her away. After a rocky start, the two grew close and, after many soul-searching debates, had secretly worked together to create the experimental shampoo and bodywash. They acted as conspiring sisters to produce a concoction that, going deeper than hair and skin, would "inspire" men. A fragrant icebreaker. It would help build confidence in those who needed it. Of course, if successful, it would be quite a boon for the company's finances as well.

Aoife had initially participated only to prove her friend wrong, to prove that men went first and foremost for appearances, and she'd heaped a $10,000 cherry on top. Cyrena had agreed to the bet as long as she could choose the testing venue. She hadn't been able to come—some kind of last-minute family emergency—but she'd sworn to be waiting when Aoife disembarked. At this point, if successful, Aoife would introduce her to the man deemed the best catch on the ship. Aoife had been emailing her daily notes in the meantime. This evening's journal entry, she knew, would take a darker tone.

The effects of the wash's chemicals were getting to her. That had to be it. A side effect . . . Or was it the unfamiliar environment? She'd never been on a cruise before, let alone one of this nature. There were too many variables, but she needed to figure it out soon and make a correction. The blackouts were not acceptable.

Weary, exhausted, and crusty eyed, she exited the closet and made her way down the passageway, back toward the club. Rotten eggs . . . rotting seaweed . . . the stench reached her nostrils well before she could imagine what was happening. When she registered the screams, her thoughts painted a more vivid picture. Moments later, at the edge of the passage, her eyes filled in the details.

It was night now, and the club had become the site of a grand feast—all dining and dancing. But there were no men, only women: severed, collapsed, broken apart. Pandemonium engulfed those still living, with their torn and shredded clothes, raw and lacerated skin. They ran in circuitous paths, attempting to defend, hide from, or otherwise escape the gray, slick-bodied creatures with agile legs and arms that appeared to be elongated, serrated flippers.

Her feet rooted, Aoife swayed as if a subtle breeze pushed her. Her mind was a near blank as she gazed at the grotesque spectacle of viscous creatures chasing shrieking victims, slapping at them, ripping fabric or skin. Out of the clamor it was hard to pick out any distinct sounds, yet her head snapped to the left when she heard a gratingly familiar tone.

Jean was half-naked and bloody but still on her feet. She'd

somehow managed to keep free of the frenzy, perhaps by hiding. Perhaps she'd found an opportunity to flee and had emerged only to find all her routes blocked. Maybe that's what prompted the scream—or maybe it was what had blocked her. The gray creature had gotten a firm hold on both her shoulders. On its shoulders were the tattered remnants of a sports jacket . . . Gareth's.

The full realization struck Aoife as Jean screamed at the top of her lungs, her head thrust back, her whole body shaking. It all only seemed to help the creature as "he" thrust his head back. The lower jaw remained close to the chest as the upper half of the head unhinged. An appendage—like a giant, mutated earthworm bulging with violet veins—erupted outward, arcing directly down into the woman's mouth. Jean stopped screaming, started gagging, and continued struggling. Her jolting movements now seemed to be more a reaction to the ejected organ working its way down her bulging neck. Her skin repeatedly expanded and compressed, like a balloon blown by an asthmatic, until reaching an equilibrium. It then rippled and bubbled as the vasiform appendage bloated. Stuff was moving through—from the inside of the woman to the inside of the man. Juices, organs . . . *Men are just stomachs . . .*

Jean's body shrunk and collapsed in on itself. His feast complete, Gareth detached, retracting the vein-bulged intestine inside himself as the desiccated skin-sack of bones fell to the floor. He then made straightaway for the nearest wall, pushing his entire body against a large pinkish-green whorl. The patch absorbed him, swallowing him from sight.

The disappearance was a slap to Aoife's face, causing her to release the fiercest scream of her life, a cry of unfiltered anguish. The ink-black eyes of every creature fell on her. They began to converge.

She couldn't find the sounds for *help*, couldn't even

conceive of a coherent utterance. Her subsequent vocalizations were as erratic and frantic as her running, which would not have formed a straight path even if furniture and other inanimate objects hadn't been in the way. Her enemy feet tipped her to the floor twice before she reined them in and made them speed up as they carried her away from the club area.

Aoife barreled into one of the ship's public rooms and stumbled several feet before catching herself on a knee and palm. She began to push herself back up, then paused. In here was the same carnage. The same creatures and the same luminescent patterns, now wider than a trio of men. She scrambled on hands and knees until she could get to her feet and bolt for the door. She had made it only two steps—almost tripping again—when two creatures dropped from the ceiling, from a psychedelic pattern above the doorway. She cut right, her peripheral vision telling her there were fewer objects in that direction, less resistance.

Her thoughts were a frazzle; her eyes threatened to dim everything within sight. Her body wanted to shut down, give in, and succumb. But she wouldn't allow it. She had to get away, get free, get safe. And she'd force her body to follow suit, even if she had to collect a few more cuts and bruises. So she ran, threading through chaos.

She only stopped when she slammed chest first into the railing.

Lifeboats. Her instincts had brought her to the level that housed the lifeboats. But there weren't any. At some point after they'd set sail, apparently, the crafts had all been released. Aoife's entire body heaved, ready to cry out again. Behind her, she heard an ethereal moaning. She spun around to see a slime-skinned gray creature emerging from the orange-brownish whorl on the floor.

She dashed for the life jackets on the wall. Five more creatures had appeared by the time she'd fastened one over her tattered jumpsuit. The creatures formed a semicircle around her. Gareth was in the middle.

Aoife's eyes locked with his. He betrayed no recognition. Something within her clicked. She snarled and barreled straight toward him.

The next moment was a blur. Yet as her body fell from the railing, Aoife pondered whether she'd evaded and just slipped on the slime or Gareth had simply stepped aside.

SHE WAS DROWNING, or so she thought before her eyes opened. There was water as far as the eye could see, but Aoife's head remained above it. *Still alive. Safe* . . . but her eyesight might have deteriorated.

It was daytime. The smeared disk above, however, cast a pinkish-green pallor over everything. Maybe it was the time of day, or maybe that was just how things were in the middle of the ocean. Rather than fret, she considered herself lucky no sharks or other man-eaters had gotten to her.

She repositioned her body, turning around. At a decent distance, perhaps a nautical mile, she saw a large mass. No sign of sand—only cliffs and jutting rocks edged it. Yet beyond the shore, there was no mistaking all the red, green, purple, and orange, betraying exotic, luxuriant vegetation. A grand heap of dangerous beauty. Was this it? La Isla? Whether it was or not, it wouldn't do her any good if there were no means on it to contact another human being.

Aoife wondered how long she could survive before a ship spotted her. *If one ever comes* . . . None other than the one she'd been on came anywhere near the island's supposed location, assuming what she'd read about the island was true. She repositioned, turning back around. It appeared the literature had a few inaccuracies—thankfully.

Where there'd been nothing before, she saw a bulb on the horizon. It was getting closer but also seemed—even from a distance—to be moving erratically. It zigged to the left, zagged to the right, and pulsed forward. She chalked it up to her dizziness, tricks of perspective, and perhaps a touch of seasickness. The important thing was that it was approaching. Soon enough, she could even make out the shape of it. She recognized the outline, the colors.

It was the same vessel she'd escaped. But it was no longer a ship.

As it neared in its abbreviated serpentine manner, she thought she could make out eyes, hot-pink orbs peering in her direction from under a midnight-blue, silvery-green carapace. Inversely to her, the bulk of the monster seemed to be above water. Part giant turtle, part whale, part scaly lizard—it incorporated yet defied the attributes of all.

It hit her like an acid-filled balloon, a malicious joke tossed straight at her face. All along, she'd misinterpreted the men's looks. Their smiles. Their attentions. Their intentions. She knew she'd escaped too easily. The creatures hadn't been interested in her as food, as fuel. Their master had only been interested in getting her into position as it revealed its true self.

More out of morbid curiosity than anything, she turned around. It was foolish to imagine she could somehow make it to the island and just as foolish to think she'd be safe there. For the island now trembled, shimmied, and shimmered, its vibrant colors even more so. She heard no unusual sounds, but she understood the signs of a mating ritual when she saw them.

She turned back around to gaze at the oncoming freak of nature, the approaching god who'd taken the form of a fully functioning ship. It had gathered and converted a crew of worshippers and had bided its time with back-and-forth voyages till it found The One to lure its queen out of hiding. As it loomed, she stared it down—fearlessly. Let the two incongruities meet and mate, and let her be a part of it.

When the leviathan opened its mouth, bringing total darkness to her world, her life, Aoife couldn't help but laugh freely. Cyrena considered herself a supreme matchmaker. If only her friend could see her now.

BEARDED MEN

My fiancée-mandated therapist hadn't exactly said that, to fix my relationship problems, I should join up with a cult. After all, Sanctuaries for the Distressed sounded like a noble charity filled with noble beings doing noble things for the downtrodden. But him describing the organization as full of "singularly obsessed men devoted to the ideas of the SFD" raised a red flag.

That crimson warning tore free from its pole to fly even higher when a gaggle of bushy-bearded men mobbed my gangly self shortly after I'd departed the Greyhound, *yawping* all the while as they hoisted me and my luggage above their shoulders, only to toss us into a waiting van.

The cackling driver floored the accelerator, thrusting the van out of the lot like a mad bull and leaving me to bounce around the leather seats like a die in a Pop-O-Matic before I managed to fasten my seat belt.

The wild-bearded men who'd piled in with me continued to yawp as the equally hirsute driver whisked us down gravel and dirt roads, weaving us past malodorous fields, dense with cows and their patties, before heading into a forest with more than a good share of skunk cabbage.

I tried asking that they roll up the windows, but between all the yawping and semi-intelligible words that sounded like "welcome," "fun," "glad," and "happy," I don't think they heard me. I was fairly certain I'd been inadvertently recruited into a pack of men who habitually raised frothy toasts to the moon and howled at everything else.

Sanctuaries for the Distressed was an organization dedicated to the idea that true lovers mired in stressful jobs and nerve-racking home lives needed a second home, a place ensconced in relative simplicity with hardly any distractions, a sanctuary where they had little to do but devote all their attention to their significant other.

Lovers in desperate need sent in applications, detailing their woes, and the lucky few selected by the organization got a luxury getaway cabin built for them at a fraction of what it would cost if they'd hired any other homebuilders.

Abiding by the solicitous guidance of my frohawked therapist, I'd applied, been accepted, and was directed to a site where the building of a glorified vacation home for some deserving amorous pair was already in progress.

The screwy van ride concluded at a clearing where a party was already in progress. I heard psychobilly music, saw grills and coolers interspersed among the few dozen men—all men, bedecked in plaid shirts and jeans—talking and laughing with one another. Here were men of various heights, ethnicities, and builds. I was the only clean-shaven one in sight.

Many approached the van as I stepped out, pressing forward to shoulder-clasp and hug me. I heard "Welcome, Brother" so many times, I briefly thought I'd wandered into a mirror world where all my siblings from alternate realities had gathered to commune. All their jostling brought me closer to a grill sizzling weird sausages that released savory aromas of unidentifiable fruits and meats, exercising my salivary glands as I watched the smoke curlicuing up, dispersing into the azure heavens.

That was the moment I realized I'd made a wise choice. I could really get along here. I was between jobs anyway—why not wholeheartedly give this a chance? It'd be like a summer camp, except happening in spring.

I relaxed and mingled, threw off a few *yawps* myself, and life began to get a little easier.

Many of the men owned RVs; those who didn't bunked with those who did. I accepted the invitation to take up space in one of the bigger vehicles with Jourt, Kelly, and Mickelson. Our encampment of recreational vehicles was within walking distance of the site.

After five days of waking up to a dewy, pine-scented morn, indulging in breakfasts of cinnamon coffee, fresh fruit, and oatmeal, only to be serenaded by chipping sparrows as we wound our way down the dirt pathways littered with long-dead pine needles so we might make a little more progress on the luxury cabin, it all began to feel like my home away from home. And the men, truly *Brothers*.

Though my therapist hadn't made the "how" of it explicit (as I was supposed to figure it out on my own), I was certain my experience here would repair my relationship with my dear Loutica. Almost a week in, I'd figured enough by this point to realize that working with one's hands in the open air, laboring to build a sanctuary for deserving others, allowed one's mind to spread its own wings, alighting on fresh ideas on how one might become a better person before returning home. Someone worthy of a lifelong mate.

When the Brothers weren't working or hanging around the encampment—innocuously chatting, seriously grilling, nursing occasional wounds, and telling piffle stories—we made excursions into the nearest small town, a short van or truck ride away, usually ending up at one or more of four destinations: the hardware store, the pharmacy, the grocery, and Wiley's Bar.

A contingent of us hit up Wiley's every day shortly after quitting the work site. Like much of the town, the bar had a laid-back, conservative vibe. Most folks this time of year were garbed in some combination of hoodies, jeans, and puffer vests. We always wore our plaid button-downs, sleeves rolled up to our elbows.

Entering during the early evening of my seventh day, I followed my routine, directing myself straight to the main concern while my fellows made their way to the dancing area and began doing their usual thing, each of them on their own.

As I planted myself on a stool near the middle, Chevy, the bartender, met my eyes and bobbed his chin upward. I nodded back. Good guy. He knew my go-to.

I looked over my shoulder toward the dance floor. As it always did within five minutes of the Brothers entering, the music had changed from modern country pop to rockabilly, and each of my fellow toilers had been joined by at least one female partner. All of them pretty young things—while my Brothers were decidedly not. The same scene, every evening. Shaking my head, I muttered, "How do they do it?"

"It's them beards." Chevy placed my gin and tonic on a coaster in front of me. "Those chin warmers, something about them charms the ladies. Gets them dancing. Can't figure it. Don't argue it."

I wasn't sure what argument I could make. I'd remained clean shaven during my time here and hadn't heard one negative word about it from the Brothers. After sipping some gin, I rubbed my bare chin, weighing the pros and cons of me growing some facial hair during my sojourn.

Then *she* blew in.

The sound of the inward swinging door smacking someone in the face turned my head; her moss-green mini dress easily caught my eye, pulling it away from her victim; and those legs . . . They mesmerized me as she stumbled about like an ambulant rag doll emerging from a washing machine that had just completed its final cycle.

I couldn't take my eyes off her, mostly because I was unable to fathom why she'd be wearing knee-high white go-go boots.

The woman had frazzled hair that looked like half a lion's mane and a (hopefully) sprayed-on tan that gave her the same hue as a toasted carrot. Two fingers on her left hand clutched the handle of a metallic blue water bottle that swung like a lantern in a windstorm as she clomped around, winding her way around tables, bumping into patrons, careening off columns. She seemed to be heading in my direction —indirectly.

I'd wager the Corvette I planned to buy someday that the blue bottle had very little water in it.

I'd also admit that the woman was alluring but stewed like a . . . Well, I still couldn't get over that carrot tan of hers, just as she almost couldn't get over the low step separating the bar area from the seating area.

The tip of her boot nicked the edge and she stumbled forward, heading in a surprisingly direct route to the empty stool on my right. She managed to catch herself before impact and straightened up, only to collapse her bottom on the stool like a dropped sack of potatoes.

I thought her head would hit the bar in a similar manner.

Instead, she whipped her face in my direction. I glanced from her squinting eyes to Chevy, who'd vamoosed to the far end of the bar and turned his back to us. I glanced her way again only to find her still gawking at me, her eyelids still indecisive about letting her eyes have some rest. I tried to focus on my drink, but I felt that hot breath hitting my cheek as if a bellows was forcing it my way.

"So what's your whine, chief?" She sounded like she'd a rock tumbler caught in her throat. Her breath smelled like boiling cabbage.

But I couldn't allow myself to be rude. Nor could I simply leave and attempt to go into hiding. The SFD was going to be in the vicinity for a while, and I liked this bar. Plus, I had the sneaking suspicion she might be as much of a fixture as the lights over the bar counter; she was certainly more lit.

I faced her, getting a fuller look at those tired lids of hers, hiding periwinkle irises caught in a bloodshot storm. Rather than recommending sunglasses and a fusillade of breath mints, I simply smiled and eloquently uttered, "What?"

Her lips sagged into a frown. "Your *whine*, you *scoundrel*."

I'm sure my face pinched into all manners of expressions as I looked over her shoulders and mine, checking to see whether the bar's décor had suddenly switched to that of one from the Old West.

Perhaps sensing my bewilderment, she went on to slur-ringly ask, "You're with the Sancs, right? I know about them. *All* about them. All allegedly working out problems with their wives or girlfriends or other significant others. Growing beards as they work on themselves while working to help others—as if they're even thinking about them . . ." She trailed off as her head turned, seemingly searching for her misplaced water bottle. I was about to indicate that she was still holding it in her left hand, the one attached to the arm that dangled at her side, but before I could open my mouth, she opened hers, letting the bottle fall as she yelped for the bartender's aid.

Despite initially having his back to our sordid scene, Chevy scampered over at her beck. I'd a faint hope he was going to tell her she'd had enough. Instead, he took her order for a diamond-back with such zest that I thought he might be charging her triple the price with no argument.

Her order in process, she turned her attention back to me. "So you with those con artists or not?"

"Uh . . . I . . ." I shook my head to rid it of the illest first responses. "I am assisting them with the construction project, yes. But—"

"So where's your beard? Don't you have something to hide like the rest of those snake handlers?"

My teeth clenched as I broke eye contact. I was all for patronizing the inebriated (when safe to do so), but when they started bad-mouthing people who'd embraced me as one of their own for no reason, who'd treated me so well for no good reason? Condescension had its necessary limits.

"No, I *don't* have something to hide. And neither do they. I don't see them as cons. Snake handling or otherwise."

"So you don't see how other women are drawn to them? And how they're not pushing those women away?"

Quite the opposite, it was true. My Brothers danced with women who invited themselves, and hardly any were shy about it. Some danced with two or three women at once. They didn't refuse any advances. Even when some of the folks outside our clique tried to cut in or break it up, they were gently rebuffed— by the women—and they took it like lambs, perhaps assured their girlfriends or wives or whatever would return to their sides when it was time to pay the check and go home. Such assurance was buttressed by experience.

All I could say, almost involuntarily, was "It's easy to get lonely out here. Besides, they don't mean anything by it. They're just having fun, working off steam after working on construction all day. And anyway, since I'm over here—*alone*— I'm clearly not like them." I emphasized *alone* in a way that I hoped conveyed my preference for the status.

The woman snorted. "See alike. Be alike."

"What's that supposed to mean?"

"You're telling me you don't go for the pretty young things?"

"I do not. I have a fiancée, who happens to be almost forty. I just turned thirty-one."

The bartender placed her drink on the bar in front of her, but she ignored it, using her eyes to give me a head-to-toe reassessment. As she did, her lips curled, perhaps a reaction of her confusion; mine curled into a smile, a smug (I admit) self-congratulation at not submitting to her sexist expectations. I had her now. I sipped my drink and decided to keep it going.

"My fiancée's ready to start a family. I'm not so sure I am. But she says she's been feeling the urgings, has been for some time. I've been told—repeatedly—the clock begins ticking at age twenty-eight or so. Is that right? Do you remember that happening with you?"

A gardener could've had a seed party with the furrows that appeared on her brow. Her lips momentarily twitched before revealing teeth ready to chew glass. "I am *twenty-five*."

I think I swallowed at least twenty times before remembering and reaching for my drink, ensuring the next few gulps were less dry.

"And," she continued, "it sounds to me that you're not ready for any kind of commitment. Your fiancée thinks she's running out of time. And here you are—*running*."

She sounded much less inebriated than before. Anger

perhaps had sobered her right up. Before it got her to do anything else, I tried to defuse.

"Me coming here was her idea. I mean, I had her blessing after our therapist recommended it. And it's only for a limited time. One month, six weeks, tops. By then, I'll have found myself. At least enough to know whether I'm ready for kids, marriage, in whatever order."

She snorted again and turned her attention to her drink. "You'll end up just like the rest of them," she muttered.

I initially thought the crack was directed at me. But she'd downed the drink in the time it took me to blink, and I'd more than an inkling that wasn't out of her norm.

I took much more time to admonish myself. *Never* try to guess or reference a woman's age. I *knew* that. I'd been raised on such wisdom. But, of course, a bar setting would render me stupid.

As if to underline my new mental state, I turned to the woman again, prepared to ask her name. She was ready for me, flashing a toothy grin before thrusting her face toward mine.

I swiveled my head to the right, allowing her to plant a big wet one on my left cheek. My head, almost on its demon-possessed own, snapped one-eighty degrees, perhaps to force my eyes to look for the exit, but in the short term allowing the woman to plant another sloppy smooch on my right cheek.

I stumbled off my stool, maintained my footing by luck, and by sheer will forced my frame into a soldier's posture as I faced her while bearing a tortured half grin, half grimace.

She regarded me with lazy eyes but no longer appeared the least bit soused. Rather, she peeped me in much the same manner as a goddess might consider a penitent worshipper who'd uttered only one line of interest in a twelve-line prayer.

Easing herself off her stool, she turned a shoulder and

slinked away without another word, making her way toward the entrance without contact with anyone or anything.

Something about the way she moved her hips made me feel too ashamed to wipe away the traces of her clumsy kisses, even though I was no longer in her sight and even though my cheeks tingled as if they'd been splattered with snowballs.

She must've entranced Chevy as well. He didn't say one word about payment for her drink until I was ready to pay for mine.

SHORTLY AFTER MY encounter with the barfly, I returned to my trailer, showered, and leafed through a few architectural magazines to send myself to sleep, subconsciously homing in on the heart of myself while trying to keep out all would-be invaders. *What did I learn about myself today?* was the usual interrogator. Tonight, I added, *What did I learn about myself this evening?* I had no answers—other than I was supremely weirded out by the strange woman.

I slept a dreamless sleep and awoke feeling as if I had the mumps. Not all the symptoms. Only the swollen jaw and puffy cheeks. But all or half, I could do without any of it.

I rushed from my bunk to the bathroom, almost giving myself the Heimlich with the edge of the sink as I thrust my face inches from the mirror, gazing close.

My face wasn't puffy or even tender to my fingertips. However, peering closer, my skin was slightly discolored as if maybe someone had been slapping me silly while I slept. I shrugged, as that was all I could do, and began to get myself ready for the day.

By the time the crew and I were making our way to the site, my discomfort was a memory.

The luxury cabin was coming into its own. A cozy one-bedroom affair with a spacious living area, fantastic porch, space for a jacuzzi and an outdoor hot tub. We had a ways to go till completion, but it was taking shape to the degree that less and less was left to the imagination. Yet among all the hammering and sawing and yawping, I imagined another party was among us today.

I listened to my instincts, looking this way and that until I spotted her. Not too distant, on the higher end of a slope, the woman from the bar lurked next to a Virginia pine. She'd doffed the mini dress and go-go boots for a sari featuring intricate patterns. The sun's light sieved through the trees' branches and, reaching her, conspired with the breeze to make that mane of wild hair flow about her head like fire burning in lesser gravity. It was difficult to tell from my position, but all the while, she seemed to glare at me without blinking.

Mickelson sidled up to me and tapped my hard hat. "Problem, Brother?"

I faced him and, with my eyes, gestured toward the woman. "Who is that?"

"Hmm?" His eyes followed mine. "Oh, that's Dandrea. I was wondering when she'd get here."

"You've seen her before? What is she, some kind of deranged groupie or something?"

"She's a project manager."

"For whom?"

"For *us*."

I was dumbfounded. Why would this Dandrea have so much contempt for us? Didn't she think the men did a good job?

I shrugged it off and got back to work, watching her surreptitiously, noting her eyes never strayed from me. Whatever her beef with the other guys, it was clear she had a mad-on for me. Probably due to the inadvertent crack I'd made about her age.

My pondering must've sent me wandering too close to someone using a circular saw. I heard the yelling a split moment after I got a face full of sawdust. Thank goodness for my helmet and safety glasses. Thank goodness twice that my mouth was closed at the time. One of the Brothers—thoughtfully yet unnecessarily—helped me to a hand-wash station. Even after I washed the dust off, the skin was still a little itchy but nothing too bothersome. It just meant I would need to take a shower and lotion up before heading to Wiley's later.

I DIDN'T SEE Dandrea around the site after the incident, nor at the bar later. Though I went to bed that evening somewhat relieved, I awoke with a milder version of the same symptoms as yesterday.

I took a little more time getting to the mirror only to gape and stand stone still when I did. The lower third of my face glistened. I had expected stubble but now wondered who had glitter bombed me. A good towel-rubbing proved that it wasn't sweat or easily removed. I'd heard of men going prematurely gray—but *silver?*

I hopped in and out of the shower and, after drying, saw that my stubble had lost its sheen. It was now more of a grayish-blackish—a fine ash that my razor would soon consign to the sink.

After lathering up real good, I lined the blade up with the middle of my right ear and began a downward stroke. I hadn't slid the razor more than a quarter of an inch before stopping to suck in air through clenched teeth. *Blood.* A fine line steadily growing less so.

Pushing expletives through my still-gritted pearly whites, I snatched a cloth from the ring, dampened it, and blotted away the red.

I rinsed the straight razor and tried again, this time on the left side of my face. This time I managed to bite my lip when piercing my skin—again after sliding the razor no more than a fraction of an inch.

"Problems?" Jourt called from the kitchen area.

"Defective razor," I yelled back, dabbing away at the two red streaks seeking to boldly underline my ineptitude at a simple morning routine.

It was an amateurish juggling act to keep dabbing while retrieving, unwrapping, and applying the adhesive bandages Mickelson kept in the medicine cabinet. For whatever reason (likely frugality), he'd only purchased bandages in one size—the length of my middle finger—with colorful, graffiti-esque designs. Upon application, I looked like a freaky clown pioneering new territory in facial art.

I spent five minutes pondering whether I could be bothered to attempt the razor on my chin or upper lip. Rather than tempt fate, I decided to just try again tomorrow.

THE MEN TOOK it surprisingly easy on me. Here, I thought, was real acceptance. Just as they initially hadn't cared whether I had a beard, they didn't care whether my face looked like it had gotten into a scrap with a surly squirrel, so long as I was hearty, happy, and ready to work.

The next day, I went at the fuzz with a better razor I'd procured from the pharmacy, yet I fared no better. My skin was just too sensitive. I emerged from the bathroom a patchwork of scruff and bandages—and with the number I had to apply this time, I must've looked like I was either getting worse at shaving or better with my clown-school lessons.

"Don't know why you persist in doing that, man," Kelly muttered to me at the site. "Makes you look a little . . . you know."

Yeah—mentally unwell. I got it.

"Just let it grow, bro. Look at us. *Join* us."

I slept on his words. And I greeted the next morning by saying to heck with it. Kelly was right. Forget trying to torture the follicles and let them do as they would, sprouting curly off-black strands. Let them grow wild and free like my Brothers'. Jourt even hipped me to the balmy leave-in conditioner he used for his whiskers. By day four, I had a nice little short beard going.

When I accompanied the Brothers to Wiley's now, I went straight to the dance floor, dancing by myself at first, only to eventually draw one partner—sometimes two, and even occasionally three, concurrently. Whenever my Brothers and I were ready to retire from the floor and indulge in our respective poisons, the women invariably unattached themselves, returning to their steadier partners or friends. So it went every evening. Not on a one of them did I see Dandrea amble in.

I did see the strange woman from time to time, appareled in a sari and walking—dangerously yet gracefully—with bare feet on the work site. On each such occasion, she seemed far more interested in the progress of the cabin than in me. She spoke briefly with some of the men, business matters only, no chitchat from what I could overhear. I was uncertain whether the version of her I'd seen in the bar was an aberration or she had just found other spots in the area to have her evening fun.

Of one thing I was certain: the damned beard was itching like crazy. Like a wool sweater hanging from my chin. Every morning. The conditioner Jourt had given me was only to be applied post-shower, and while it got me through the day, it didn't always last through the night. The irritation inspired some bizarre dreams. Even when I made it peacefully through the night, I woke up to an almost unbearable prickling and tickling.

Had to be a medical condition. Beard dandruff, perhaps.

After a day's work, before joining my Brothers at the watering hole, I swung by the pharmacy to put in a special order for a medicated shampoo specifically for beards. The pharmacist said he wasn't sure there was such a thing, but he'd look into it. He also suggested that I, in the meantime, try a new comb.

I found one I liked, a fine-toothed implement that seemed really promising for untangling knots and getting at the crumbs my current comb couldn't. Heading to the checkout counter, I passed through the eyewear section. I had no use for reading glasses, but the magnifying glass I spotted might be useful for getting to the root of the issue.

I awoke the next morning much like I had on recent mornings: madly hustling to the bathroom for my shower and beard balming. Before applying the conditioner, however, I remembered the magnifying glass.

Retrieving it from my bag, I returned to the bathroom, holding it aloft like some sort of torch of truth. *I'll seek out and smoke out those annoying little particles.*

I placed the glass between my beard and the mirror. My eyes widened, watching the hairs swaying. Animated by the shower water and as-yet uncalmed by the balm—maybe that's how facial hair worked? Maybe this was one of the manly secrets my father had neglected to pass along to me, like how to tie a necktie or pass a football or down half a cup of straight scotch without one's throat erupting in flames. But the swaying hairs . . . Was it normal for them to each waver in their own way?

I pressed the glass closer to my beard. As I squinted—drilling down—my mouth widened this time, perhaps in awe or perhaps subconsciously hoping to find words to whisper back to what I now saw as thousands upon thousands of swaying, curling, twisting, writhing hairlike serpents, each of them having their source in my follicles, each of their tongues flickering as they hissed nearly subaudible whispers like a breeze weaving through tall grasses.

Needless to say, I was entranced. Needless or not, I'm not sure I could've said anything anyway. I could only gape like a Gorgon, the nature of the Brothers' true bond gradually dawning on me.

For who knows how many minutes, I did not move. Couldn't, as the minuscule serpents' language became somewhat coherent to me. They imparted a long-kept-secret knowledge (long kept from me, anyway): I wasn't fit for my fiancée; I wasn't fit for any serious relationship; I was only fit for constructing sanctuaries—being a man of brick and wood and stone.

At some point, I pulled myself away from the mirror—or was more likely pulled away by Jourt or Kelly needing to use the facilities and preferring some privacy while doing so. Regardless, I managed to finish dressing, then accompanied my fellows to the work site, pondering only what I might like to eat for lunch later.

In a few weeks' time, the cabin was complete and ready for occupancy. Members of our bushy-bearded Brotherhood lined either side of the pea-gravel walkway leading to the front porch, where Dandrea stood, bearing the key and ready to give the new owners their first look and a grand tour of their vacation love shack.

I stood about in the middle of the line on the left. As the couple crunched past me, I could swear the woman looked awfully familiar. "Utica" something? I also thought I recognized her frohawked partner. But once they disappeared behind the front door, I forgot them both.

Our work here was done. Time to pack up the RVs and move on to the next site.

LOVE HAX

The smooth sax and subtle piano of soft jazz filled the apartment the moment Breskva eased the front door shut behind her. The sound system had been designed to begin gently serenading the couple once the key bearer and the pretty young thing he'd brought with him were safely inside the premises. It was perhaps too much to expect the system to be smart enough to recognize a wiser woman entering alone, after having picked the lock.

She declined to lock the door; no need to trigger the hidden cameras. She likewise declined to flick the switch next to the door, turning off the music. Instead, she cast glances left and right, through both entryways, seeing only sharp edges of a dining table in the room to her right and an empty hallway to her left. The visual check was partly out of habit; despite the lack of total silence, she had a much better chance of hearing someone coming before she saw them. The quick gander to either side worked more as a coin toss. *Which way through the labyrinth?*

Directly in front of her stood a chest-high black hourglass

with a hexagonal top surface, an object perhaps originally intended as an end table. Here, it stood alone, displaying a modest glass vase filled with sticks—a bouquet that had forgotten to bud, let alone flower. Breskva allowed her eyelids to get lazy as she took a sustained breath. Sage and basil. Rosewood. Jasmine. The average infrequent visitor would take in the combined scents, and she—it was almost always a "she"—would immediately get the sense that she was in the presence of class and elegance before she even laid eyes on anything else in the apartment's interior. The visitor would shrink into her best, most compliant behavior. Breskva only gagged.

To keep from retching all over the floor, she held her breath as she bent down to remove her leather pumps. With bucket bag slung over her shoulder, she proceeded into the dining room, eyes passing briefly over the charcoal-gray furniture to quickly survey the area. No walls separated the dining from the adjacent kitchen and living areas.

Her bare feet were quiet on the hardwood flooring, which didn't feel as cold as she'd expected. Perhaps some of that could be chalked up to her calluses; the rest could be attributed to the apartment being on the sixth floor. The open vertical blinds of the floor-to-ceiling windows at the far end may have provided some warmth as well, despite the fact the sun was continuing its midmorning ascent beyond their view.

Everything in her line of view was sleek, contemporary— from the furniture to the knickknacks and sculptures adorning them. Modern art filled negative spaces on the walls. Pricey stuff from artists who were still living and whose works would remain comfortably unrecognized by anyone who would ever sleep in a place like this. The items guaranteed to draw the most attention, however, were among the smallest; they were also perhaps the most confounding to any who tried estimating their value based on mere surface appearances. Two of the silver spheres rested on the mantelshelf.

She retrieved her gloves from her bucket bag. Sliding them on, she cast one more look at the rectangular dining table, stifling a guffaw with a quick head shake. At its center rested a nest woven with pussy willow stems and filled with artificial bird's eggs, their hues ranging from bashful baby blue to blushing pink to an embarrassed, fading yellow. The nerve of having an Easter-themed centerpiece here. How could one even imagine straight faced a sacred or familial dinner of any kind in a place like this? There was audacity in having such a dining table at all. *Eight chairs* . . . As if more than two, maybe three, would ever be occupied at once. Sense, if not decency, would call for downsizing the table to a circle, if not a triangle.

As she neared the mantelshelf, Breskva reached for the first sphere. A voice stopped her.

Gently she closed her eyes and listened as the husky songstress threaded French lyrics through the smooth jazz. The music was no longer possible to ignore. Its volume hadn't increased. It remained at a level low enough not to drown out any of the casual words spoken by living-yet-impermanent lovers. But it was the voice. That sultry voice. Impossible to forget once danced to more than a dozen times.

Before they'd married, Serge had introduced her to the vocal wonders of the late-twentieth-century French chanteuses. At one time, it was the only music guaranteed to draw them into an embrace, but his tastes eventually moved on. Incorporating such music into the properties' sound systems had been her idea. Years ago. By now, she'd thought the company's tastes might have moved on as well.

As she swayed to the music, a mélange of scents wafted her way. A mix of lavender and rose. Lemon, verbena, and bergamot. Sandalwood and oak moss. Class, *elegance*. Though she knew better, she couldn't help but let the environment take her, much as it had done with many women. She fell into it. And if any man happened to be here with her, she'd fall into his arms without a care.

Her tongue moistened. She tasted iron. *Blood.*

Her body was reacting—just as she had prepped it to. She opened her eyes and checked her watch. She still had at least an hour, but she couldn't afford any more dallying.

She grabbed the first silver sphere from the mantelshelf and examined it quickly before retrieving from her bag a red cloth with a "1" printed in its corners. She wrapped the sphere in the soft cloth and gently placed it in the bag. Using a red cloth marked with a "2," she followed the same process for the second sphere, then turned around, looking every which way for any she might have missed. Satisfied, she proceeded to the glass door leading to the covered terrace.

There were three spheres here. They and another vase of incense sticks adorned the patio table. Only two spheres were silver. The transparent one didn't interest her.

She retrieved a yellow cloth from her bag and followed the same process as before. As she lifted the second sphere, she paused, hearing a *plink-plink* from the metal doorframe behind her. She turned, landing her gaze on a man standing in the open doorway.

Attired in a stylish blazer and eye-catching tie, the man with the high fade and loose pompadour at first seemed exactly like the sort who'd entertain a woman here—except he was half her age rather than the other way around. And with his natural baby-faced looks distorted by his eyebrows squishing together, he seemed far removed from the mood to entertain.

"Breskva?"

She forced a smile. "Hi, Gerald."

"What are you doing here?"

"I, uh—"

"I'm *showing* this property in thirty minutes."

She tried not to lose her smile as she ground her teeth. Kendee had screwed up the schedule. *Again.* "I, uh, just wanted to get some ideas for my next showing."

"What next showing? Certainly not anywhere around here."

She didn't have an answer, and she was grateful he didn't wait for one.

"You could have pulled up images of anything you needed from our database."

"Sometimes I prefer to get up close and personal."

His glare fell to her right hand, still holding the silver sphere. "So I see."

Breskva swallowed. Her gloves could be explained. *Let's keep items smudge-free for the clients.* Beyond that, she wasn't sure she'd have the words.

Gerald didn't seem to have the patience for hearing even one.

He nodded toward the sphere. "You, uh, want to put that back? And leave?"

She returned the silver ball to its place and hoped she wasn't blushing as she neared the doorway. He stepped back and away to let her through. She hurried to the foyer, hoping to outpace any further questions he might have.

As she slid on her pumps, his final words for her turned out to be a statement.

"I'm sure this incident will come up at the next meeting."

She hoped she'd be able to come up with a serviceable explanation by then.

WHEN SHE WAS INCLINED, Breskva made some mighty powerful brews.

The peppermint and mocha notes wafting from the teacup on the patio table behind her defied the afternoon breeze, pleasing her nostrils as she leaned slightly over the metal railing, surveying the construction site across the street. More luxury condos were on the way. Progressive architecture, housing and hosting the businesses of aggressive men with regressive attitudes. *More and more.*

Six stories below, on the next block's sidewalk, an electronica musician played to a sparse and likely bemused crowd. The squawking, mewling, and hissing that reached her sounded like cats, birds, and robots all fighting to the death.

She was overdue for a getaway. A retreat to the cottage she and Serge had made into an incomplete home. It had been almost a dozen years since his passing. It had taken four or so for her to transition into a new career, but once she'd gotten her footing, she had closed deals like no other. Her years with Serge had given her increased confidence, and when she wanted, she could pour on the charm like no one else. But for the past couple of years, she hadn't been able to pull them in like she used to. She hadn't been able to get as many men to rent a property, let alone buy. Around the office, it was rumored her time was done. She'd been relegated to using her keen research methods to find potential clients, just so her younger colleagues —zealous and sly—could approach them. These young schmoozers rose in the ranks more rapidly than she had. Her fault, she knew, but she'd had no choice. The talents she'd previously used to approach clients, manipulate, and close deals had to be diverted to where they were more beneficial. Her role at the company had changed, but her history hadn't been forgotten. Not entirely. She maintained some perks. The one she valued most was the ability to work remotely.

Settling into the patio chair, she opened her laptop and keyed up her company's secure site. After entering codes on a series of log-in screens, she scanned the property listings until locating the one she'd visited this morning. She clicked the play button and skipped past the footage from the foyer and dining area, only slowing at the point where the hidden cameras had captured the renter and his pretty guest in the living area, chatting, caressing. She, in her late twenties and a little black dress. He, early fifties, in a dark blue three-piece suit, sans tie. This would be their last rendezvous—in this property, at least.

Breskva fast-forwarded through the boring parts, the parts her colleagues might find useful at some point. She slowed the recording to normal speed whenever they neared the fireplace. The two spheres on the mantelshelf looked like soap bubbles, transparent with shimmering hints of colors gliding across their curved surfaces. The spheres couldn't help but draw one's attention, impel one to physically touch, caressing them while marveling at the shifting tones.

In the video, the man took a bubble in each hand and held them aloft, allowing more light to reach them while he speculated on the objects' provenance. In all the recordings she'd viewed, Breskva had noticed that men rarely avoided an opportunity to conjure fanciful tales about the objects' history or worth—yet it was impossible to tell how many of the wide-eyed women were impressed with the words in equal measure to the sight of the bubbles filling with colors. Shades of reds, yellows, and oranges misted into the semitransparent globules as the surface dimmed, resolving into silver. What had been transparent globes became spherical mirrors, prone to giving imperfect reflections.

The man replaced the transformed spheres on the mantelshelf, then led his lady friend back to the couch where they sipped Pinot Noir and necked. If they gave them any thought at all, they undoubtedly assumed the bubbles' performance had been the result of light exposure. It was unlikely either considered fingerprints—the skin and its signatures and its oils.

Breskva noted that the mantelshelf bubbles had been turned by the man then fast-forwarded on. The couple soon moved to the covered terrace where, predictably, the young woman spotted more bubbles. She couldn't help but approach, touch, and fondle one, then another, gaping both times at the transformation. Two more nothings converted into charms.

Breskva noted the spheres from the terrace had been turned by the woman, then pushed the recording forward, viewing the footage from the bedrooms and bathrooms.

Three more bubbles had been turned in those areas. She sighed, knowing she'd need to figure out a way to retrieve those later. She didn't dare go back anytime soon, but she wasn't sure she could trust Kendee to retrieve them, adhering to a foolproof system to remember which room she'd taken them from, as she went through to stock the place with new clear bubbles. Even after a couple of years as the company's receptionist and her trained personal assistant, the redhead was still green in certain areas.

Breskva figured she'd need to write off this property for a while, then stifled a laugh, shaking her head. Such an action wouldn't make her much different from most of the men who passed through, taking up temporary residence in the properties. Players. Men of short seasons. Them and their pretty peaches . . . the pretty young women these "sophisticated" men had plucked, saving them from the dire circumstances of a low-paying job, an immature boyfriend, or simply feeling lost in a new city. These older, moneyed men picked them when they were on the verge of ripeness and treated them as they felt the women wanted to be treated—wined, dined, and adored. That is, when the men had time for it.

Serge had been a master of making time. He'd been a gallant philanderer, a charming cheater. Breskva had felt no shame in wooing the gregarious man away from his second wife. It's not like he wasn't already stepping out on her. It's not like she shouldn't have been set free the moment he flatly refused to give her the children she desired. That poor woman was more than ten years his junior. And though she claimed to love Serge—who didn't? Breskva was as convinced the unful-filled wife would be happier with someone else as she was convinced that Serge would be happier with no one other than Breskva, even if she also happened to be more than ten years his junior and had her own desires.

To the left of her laptop, her smartphone buzzed. Kendee had sent her a text, asking if she could meet for happy hour. She'd already selected a time and place.

After some hesitation, Breskva responded in the affirmative —though she doubted there'd be much joy in the get-together.

LIKE A FIVE-FOOT LAVA lamp in a darkened theater, Kendee couldn't help but draw slack-jawed interest, no matter her location. From the young and the old, the male and the female. Few who just happened to glance could resist doing a double take at the shapely twentysomething redhead who rarely remained still for more than three seconds.

At their little round table near the edge of the patio, Breskva had been doing her best to stave off unnecessary atten-tion by attempting to calm the woman who, for the past fifteen minutes, hadn't stopped squirming and gesturing as she simul-taneously tried to explain and apologize for this morning's schedule mix-up. The gin punch Kendee had ordered and quickly finished had given her extra energy. Breskva doubted she could withstand the hysterics for fifteen minutes more, let alone a full hour.

The punch garden, though, had been a good choice. The bar itself and much of the seating was under a covered patio; an adjacent grassy area provided additional seating as well as plenty of room for standing. The tropical music flowing from the speakers was kept at an inoffensive volume, and this evening's patrons seemed to be a relatively sedate after-work crowd, not the revelers sure to turn out on Friday and Saturday. Though Kendee turned quite a few heads here, none approached offering to buy her another drink. In the middle of a workweek, perhaps none wanted to risk the drama.

Kendee suddenly tossed her head back. "*Omigosh!* I just can't—!"

"*Enough.*" Breskva almost knocked her half-empty glass of rum punch off the table as she raised her hands, palms facing outward. "What's done is done. We've just got to do better next time. *Both* of us." She glanced around, then leaned in. "I'll figure out how to handle the folks at the office. In the meantime, I need you to—"

Kendee's eyes widened at the sight of something over Breskva's shoulder.

Breskva slowly turned her head. A man in his mid- to late thirties with a crop-top haircut and a puckish expression was approaching. He'd one hand in his jeans pocket; the other grasped a nearly full pint glass of beer.

Breskva returned her gaze to Kendee, who seemed two shades paler than before.

"Well, well, *well*—What am I looking at *here?*" The man stopped behind the table's remaining empty seat. "A MILF-and-young-honey situation." He set his beer on the table.

Breskva attempted to ignore him as she glowered at Kendee, who in turn lowered her chin, looking as if she wanted to crawl into herself.

"Is this seat taken?" the man asked after sitting.

Breskva reached for her glass and spoke over the rim before sipping. "Wouldn't the floor be more comfortable?"

The man cocked his head. "The floor?"

"That's where dogs are used to sitting. Though perhaps the grass over there might be more appropriate."

He snorted. "Dog, huh? Maybe one of you would like to *collar* me?"

"Not a bad idea." Breskva faced him, leaned closer. "Do you prefer a burning tire or just razor wire?"

Getting a better look at him, she admitted (to herself) that he was roguishly handsome. Not bad at all. But her smile remained forced. His, smug.

"You know, you're funny cute," he said. "That's a nice asset for women." He studied all that he could see of her, lingering on her chest. "Though not as nice as others . . ." He shifted his leer to Kendee. "How about you, red? How's your sense of humor?"

Kendee's head shook like that of a child being offered a spoonful of castor oil.

"You the silent type?"

"She's confused," Breskva said, "wondering how a discarded diaper managed to take human form."

The man's lips pursed as he reached for his beer. After swallowing a sip, he said, "That's a fascinating accent you've got. Where might you be from?"

"I might tell you, if you promise to go there. Immediately."

"Only if you'll . . . *escort* me. Maybe we could stop off at your fancy condo first for a little video streaming and whatever." He tossed a smile at Kendee. "How about the three of us?"

Kendee almost knocked her chair over as she grabbed her clutch purse and made a beeline toward either the ladies' room or the exit.

Watching her disappear behind potted plants, the man shrugged. "Guess the concept was a little too kinky for her."

"Maybe you should follow her example and make yourself scarce."

"Or, maybe . . ." He leaned closer. "I'll just stick with the mastermind here."

She grimaced before averting her eyes, casually scanning other patrons while reaching for her drink.

"Breskva Sort-a-*ledge*. Sort of a cute name there."

"Sounds a lot cuter when it's pronounced correctly." Though she wouldn't deign to pronounce *Sortilège* for him, she was somewhat impressed he'd done well with the first name. He'd had help, of course.

"Widowed. Pushing fifty. And like not a few second chancers in that age range, she's managed to find some footing in the real estate game. But, word on the street is you haven't been a very good employee, despite your fine-wine experience."

"Maybe you should sober up and vet the sources of those words."

He snickered. "You work for Diprose Realty, specializing in selling and renting out choice properties and locations for high-powered men—and some women—to have their trysts, discretion ensured. Glorified love shacks for those looking to hack their love lives. Funny, huh?"

"The humor escapes me."

"Guilt doesn't. Did you know that *Diprose* is from the names of Eros and Cupid, spelled backward and mashed together? What a laugh! An even bigger laugh is that you—despite being a trusted employee of this lucrative enterprise—would risk it all with clumsy larceny. Why?"

"I couldn't say—because I haven't stolen anything."

"They have you on tape, *Bressy*."

"Unlikely." She was always careful not to trip the cameras when entering a property—at least, not to trip the switches she knew about. What if there was a secondary trigger, one activated when it detected motion?

"Fine." He rose. "Stick to that." He lifted his glass and finished his beer. "But know that I'm sticking to you. And once I have everything I need to bring down the hammer . . ." He flashed a grin and walked away, leaving his empty glass on the table.

The humor no longer escaped her. A man, pretending to be a detective or even a cop, tipping his hand to his target. Or a potential blackmailer who didn't even push for her to open the door to an amount. Though perhaps he was the overconfident type, wanting her to have a night or two to think things over, wondering what and how much he really had on her, so that when she saw him again, she'd be willing to offer him anything —money, body, soul—to save herself. Yes, she saw the humor, all right.

And she'd be taking the rest of the week off.

BRESKVA GLANCED at the bistro chair to her left, where a sparrow had alighted, chirping and hopping across the top of the backrest. The song-and-dance routine was likely a request for a bit of the bread on the petite round table before her.

"Isn't it almost your bedtime?" Even as she said it, she was reaching for a slice. She tore off a generous portion of the crunchy crust and tossed it far from her, beyond the nearest trees.

Once the bird fluttered off, the second chair was empty

again. Breskva leaned back in hers, slowly blinking at the dimming sky above while noting the unnatural music. The jazztronica had been kept at a low volume, preventing it from carrying too far and allowing her to ignore it with minimal effort when she wanted to.

She'd set herself up in an irregular circle, its boundaries loosely demarcated by weeping cherry trees. The intermittent breeze shimmied the pink blossoms, swayed the shiny dangling spheres, and set the teardrop baubles spinning. Only on her face and hands did she feel the evening wind's caresses—as she preferred. It set the mood to the same extent that her deconstructed jumpsuit contradicted it. The outfit's denim was comfortable against her skin, much as Serge's had been when they were dating. Jean jackets had been his thing during the days when he had never been late, had never no-showed, had never argued with her or questioned her decisions. Or her mistakes. Forgiveness, back then, had been in abundance.

She had been sitting now for almost an hour, the steel cord inches from her left hand. She had no issue with waiting an hour or so more. This evening, she was sure, would not bring disappointment.

She raised her glass to her lips, paused to inhale deeply, then—after clearing her lungs—sipped. With mangoes, peaches, raspberries, and other fruits drowning in a blend of moscato, soda, and more potent liquids, the concoction had become a necessary component of spending a painless evening in this backyard approximation of a glade. She'd never been a fan of wine or of any other liquor on its own. Serge, pestering her to spend some time with him outside on an evening, had eventually enticed her by mixing up some sangria. She almost immediately fell in love with it as she initially had with him, even though she'd suspected one of his paramours had been the first to introduce the drink to him. As that evening drew on,

Breskva had more than a suspicion that the entire purpose had been to *ease* her while he ginned up the courage to tell her about one or more of his not-so-secret lovers. But that day had ended without controversy. As did the next two-person back-yard sangria party. And the next.

She'd stirred up this batch early this morning. Though she'd prepared enough for an intimate gathering, enough to keep two or three happy and close, she'd poured only one glass. Another glass remained empty, in front of the empty seat.

The two-bedroom cottage she'd once called her primary residence was more than fifty paces behind her, out of her range of vision, but it would permit no visitor without setting off bells that would raise the dead. Anyone who wanted to see her would have to meet her here, where the frogs sang.

Though they seemed mere outdoor decorations, the six amphibian sculptures were outdoor speakers, presently croaking tunes that displayed a mélange of styles, with two French singers, a male and a female, providing the occasional vocals. Concocted for the ephemeral dance clubs catering to the young and energetic, the style of music wasn't entirely her thing; after a few years, though, it was beginning to grow on her.

The music had lulled her, yet it didn't prevent her from picking up separate noises behind her, nearing.

She sipped her sangria. The springtime grass was pliant, the soil underneath soft, but the man's lead-footed gait gave his sneakers a bad name.

When he was less than a few paces behind her, she raised her voice. "*Dugo se nismo vidjeli.*"

Keeping a generous radius with her, he entered her view with a cocked head and raised eyebrow, his hands in his unzipped jacket's pockets. He stopped about a dozen paces in front of the bistro table. "Say again?"

"It means, 'Long time, no see.'" She smirked. "I've retained some of the language in addition to some of the accent."

The man snorted, then raised his chin. He clucked as he took in the trees' decorations. "Seems to me like you've been retaining all sorts of things you should have left alone. Here, on full display." He returned his gaze to her. "*Really*, Bressy baby?"

Breskva neither averted her eyes from him nor blinked as she pinched off a hunk of bread.

He maintained, until she began chewing. A muscle in his face twitched. Then another.

He blinked, rapidly, before jerking his hands from his pockets. He fumbled with the jacket's zipper before managing to zip it up to his chest.

She almost laughed at his feeble attempt to make her think he wasn't losing confidence.

He tried distraction next, nodding toward the empty glass on the table. "Do you know what they say about women who drink alone?"

"Do you know what they do to boys pretending to be licensed authorities?" She raised her glass to him. "You think you can just wander onto private property, *Tucker*?"

He sneered. "I've been deputized. Don't you worry your pretty little head about any of that. Just realize you're not in a position to tell me what I can and can't do. The police will be on my side. And you? Stealing from the company . . . And"—he chuckled—"after having learned what you Diprose clowns are *really* up to? Recording people so you can blackmail them later? Oh, *man* . . . I've got iron-clad armor." He slid his hands into his jeans pockets this time and puffed out his chest. "I can make them forget about your thievery."

"By threatening to out my colleagues to the authorities."

"Exactly."

"They won't be extorted."

"Maybe. Maybe not. But you've got beaucoup money yourself. How much are you going to pay me to leave you out of this when I go to the authorities, blow this whole scheme wide open?"

"I've already paid as much as I'm going to."

He shook his head. "You haven't paid me anything."

"I've allowed you here. Onto my property."

"I tracked you down, fine wine."

"You did?" She allowed herself a good laugh. "You . . . A between-jobs bad boy by the name of Tucker Ackermann. Unattached. No kids. In need of money—and in possession of a mind susceptible to being hacked when exposed to ludicrous get-rich-quick schemes."

Tucker's head tilted to the left as his brow furrowed.

"The one who gave you my address is the same one who, weeks ago, approached you with a fake name and credentials. The same one who, after buying you enough drinks and flashing enough cash, sold you on a scheme to play detective. You eventually agreed to be hired as such, incentivized by being made privy to all sorts of wild, crazy information. Some true, some false. None of which you can take to the bank, let alone to any reputable authorities."

"Are you *kidding*?" He stepped forward, jabbing an index finger toward her. "Do you have any idea what I have on you?"

"I know what's under you. And above you."

He paused. Slack jawed, he cast his eyes around. With sunlight almost absent, there was little he could make out on the ground, save for what the frog sculptures allowed by way of the low wattage bulbs in their eyes. Tucker spent more time gawking at the tree branches, spinning around slowly, possibly realizing that the decorations served a purpose, but not a festive one.

"You referred to me as 'widowed,'" Breskva said, "but my Serge was never dead. Not in the way you assume. He simply *passed*. His body cremated. And the remains . . . Well . . ."

She made a broad, sweeping gesture with her right arm as her left hand grasped the steel cord and jerked. Nearby, several unseen machines sputtered and revved, shaking the cherry trees, coercing them to release blossoms, silver spheres, and teardrop baubles, the decorations bursting upon impact on the trembling ground. Tucker stumbled left and right but didn't fall, nor did he run. He couldn't have even if he'd wanted to.

The contents of the broken spheres and ornaments rapidly seeped into the frightened ground and mixed, forcing it to whisper out a thick vapor—a conglomerate of scents ambiguous yet earthy, scents exotic and sensual, erotic and noxious—a suffocating vapor Tucker had no hope of grasping, let alone pushing away as it enveloped him, overtaking him.

Immune yet bothered by the spectacle—as she always was —Breskva leaned forward, watching as an engulfed, staggering Tucker gasped for air, each of his deep inhalations bringing in far more than his exhales released.

For what may have been five minutes or fifty, the vapor permeated his being until that which surrounded him began dissipating, harmlessly entering the atmosphere. Tucker continued to stumble about—hacking occasionally, sniffling more often, spitting quite a bit—until he'd calmed enough to stand in one spot, bent over, hands grasping his knees.

Eventually, he straightened—knees firm, shoulders back, eyes gleaming.

Breskva approached.

When their eyes met, he gave her a gentle smile. She couldn't help but return the expression.

Standing almost nose to nose, gazing into each other's eyes. She began to speak. "I . . ."

His smile broadened. "Yes?"

A transformation had occurred. There was a subtle light within those orbs, but the hue was off. Tucker was indeed a new man—but not her man.

She shook her head, lowered her chin to her chest. "I'm sorry."

"Thank you, anyway." He stepped backward. "*Thank* you." He bowed toward her before turning and walking back the way he'd come. By the time he returned home, he would remember none of this—but the experience would have a lasting effect.

As the sound of his footfalls faded, Breskva's eyelids drew closer together.

Some of him—but not him.

She only opened her eyes when she heard fresh footsteps nearing. Ballet flats on the grass.

Save for the frogs' eyes and the half moon that had crept from behind a cloud, they would have been in total darkness. But Kendee had managed to reach and slump into the bistro chair without stumbling over anything. She narrowed her eyes at the empty glass and practically whispered, "I'm sorry. When I first saw him a couple of weeks ago, I thought there was something there. But I screwed up ag—"

"*No.* You did fine. And you'll keep doing fine. Just keep going by your instincts."

Kendee shook her head, seeming to only hear what she wanted. "But he—"

"Is a gain. Not a loss. The obnoxiousness has been smoked out of him, at least. He'll go on to find the right woman, and they'll make a decent couple. Now, c'mon." She picked up the glasses. "Bring the bread and the pitcher. It's getting chilly out here."

Kendee did as instructed and followed her, silently, to the

cottage. Only Breskva was smiling, but once inside, after a few drinks, they'd both be.

Before Breskva had located her and gotten her a job, Kendee had been a lost girl, drifting from job to job, from residence to residence, from abusive boyfriend to substance abuse to abusive boyfriend. Breskva had placed her in a safe space and gained her trust by trusting her with the secrets of some of her own talents. She'd told her just enough to be effective. Over the past couple of years, the girl had dutifully sought out attractive young men, all a little rough around the edges. Working with a third associate, she'd done her part to position them, each time believing—if all went well—they'd simply be imbued with the spirit of Breskva's beloved. But Breskva had been anxiously waiting—and would have to wait longer still—for the day when she could surprise the young woman.

Breskva had lost her husband. She hadn't had children. And Kendee had never truly known her father. But one evening, when the hex worked just right, Serge's spirit would inhabit another, acting and speaking through them. Breskva would have the only one she'd ever loved back, in the only way she could. Kendee would have a conduit to her biological father. In turn, Serge would have a clear channel to his only child, open access to experience the best sort of love any parent could ever know. A love that would defy death.

In the meantime, Breskva would have to keep on, loving the work that got her up in the mornings: plucking the glass-metal fruit that could redeem the irredeemable.

She and Kendee would spend the remainder of the weekend at the cottage bonding and plotting, hopeful for what next week might bring.

VIOLETS ARE CRUEL

An intense scent of rose caught Blakely by surprise when he rushed through the theater's backdoor exit. A brief coughing fit further slowed his pursuit.

He had expected fresh air. He'd also expected to spend a nice Saturday afternoon at the movies with his current girlfriend, not for them to get into an argument in the middle of an unfunny romcom.

Yazmin had stormed out of the theater, undoubtedly stomping on a few toes in her path. After some hesitation, and with more care for his footsteps, he followed—though he remained unsure what he'd say to her.

He'd have more time to think about it. There was no sign of her on the red brick sidewalk on his side or across the street. No signs of anyone else either.

The late spring breeze, however, was blowing from his left, carrying Yazmin's floral perfume.

Blakely called her name as he turned into the wind, making an extra effort to breathe as he proceeded alongside a cobblestone roadway—one apparently closed to traffic.

He hadn't been on this side of the theater before—had never seen this street—but the eighteenth-century Georgian-style and nineteenth-century Victorian-style buildings were reminiscent of the historic district of a town he knew well. The home of his alma mater.

Presently, he passed the same types of establishments he'd frequented or strolled past in his college days, with a different girl on his arm each time. An antique store, a candy shop, a bookstore, a flower shop, a coffeehouse . . .

None were open for business. Odd for a Saturday afternoon.

As odd as the disappearing act the sun had pulled while he and Yazmin had been in the theater. The forecast had said nothing of rain. But the overcast sky appeared as if it had been in place for a while.

Every so often, a random drop hit upon his forehead or arms. He hadn't an umbrella and saw no place to purchase one. If the clouds suddenly opened . . .

The plants would be happy at least. A box stuffed with flowers and greenery adorned every other window he passed. To be admired by other passersby, perhaps. To Blakely, they were diversions.

Each time he picked up another hint of rose, he glanced about, searching for any sign of Yazmin while ultimately scanning the flowers, looking for any actual roses that might be misleading him.

The window boxes were as free of roses as the street and sidewalks were of people. No vehicles. No stray bicycles. The breezes carried no human chatter, no sounds of motors, not even a bird's chirrup.

The only signs of life were the flowers, all of them out of his reach, waving and bobbing in the air's currents.

Blakely wound himself through a labyrinth of narrow and

narrower streets and alleys, calling Yazmin's name, calling for a response from anyone, hoping to outpace the impending rain as he passed buildings that all looked alike, until he found himself on a street lined with squat, brightly colored buildings.

He walked slowly, an uneasy smile spreading under his nose as he observed the baby blues, the yellows, the pinks—so contrary to the brown, tan, and red-brick sameness he'd just left.

Lavender, peach, mauve . . . This was no part of the city where he now lived. This was the historic downtown area of the town in which he'd been born and raised.

An area now empty. Deserted.

Except for the violets.

In hanging baskets, in pots lining the sidewalks—nothing but violets. Yellow, white, and lavender flowers bobbing in the breeze, some seeming to wink from sight each time a cold drop of rain burst on Blakely's skin.

But they didn't disappear completely. The heart-shaped leaves were abundant here.

Here—the place he'd abandoned for a more mature life.

Springing up uninvited in lawns, wild violets were mere weeds to landscapers dedicated to uniform greenness. But to one dedicated to wonder—to one like a child—the wild ones were random instances of beauty. Or so he had felt.

Playing in yards back then, he'd run with delight and reckless abandon to each buttercup, to each daffodil, and to whatever else was out of sorts, incongruous yet beautiful on its own. Running, running, running to each. To each flash of beauty. Violets had been his favorite. *Plucking, plucking, plucking*—till his fingers were tired.

It had all caught up to him.

The rain. The hurt. The haunting of streets, searching for a spontaneous love he really didn't want and that certainly didn't want him. The living his adult life as a child, passing from one wild fling to another, plucking and discarding without a care.

In the downpour, he trudged down the middle of the street, musing on ghosts of lost loves. And loves lost.

He paid no mind to any direction. Yet the surrounding sheets of rain seemed to part here and there, steering him to a covered stoop, where he sat and rested.

Roses have led . . .

He smelled Yazmin's fragrance once more. It was followed by hints of clove, lemons and other fruits, jasmine—and culminated with violets.

The strong revenants overwhelmed his nose, his throat —*choking, choking, choking* . . .

Leaving . . .

A discarded body, as random as the rain.

THE SILVER GREEN

Deanna's pheromones were poisonous to men. That was the best answer to the questions she muttered to herself as she plodded along the rain-slicked sidewalks.

There were hardly any cars on the streets and even fewer pedestrians on the flagstone walkways lining them. The few others she did see moved quickly, possibly hurrying to an appointment, but more likely wanting to evade the wet woman who couldn't stop talking to herself.

Deanna chuckled bitterly, thinking despite how she may have appeared in their eyes, she was actually one of the driest women alive.

Having a rare day off from filming, she'd planned to begin this misnamed Sunday with a brunch date at one of the city's most exotic restaurants—a first date, and a relatively blind date, for which she'd offered to pay.

Any hint of romance dissipated before she finished her first mimosa. Soon after, she found herself walking in a drizzle without an umbrella.

How could a date with an average-looking nobody go so disastrously?

How could all her first dates go so poorly?

How could *she* be rejected so consistently?

As a successful actor in her early thirties who (according to every public opinion that mattered) was one of the prettiest women in film today, she felt she deserved a little better. If so many men all over the country were allegedly drooling over her image and concocting fantasies about her, her mere presence in the flesh should have ensured an enjoyable date.

Success at the box office clearly didn't translate to success at finding a boyfriend, or even a friend with benefits.

Over the past decade, she'd tried dating fellow actors, wealthy businessmen, and entrepreneurs who'd nothing to them but decent looks, unusual personalities, or interesting ideas. Lately, she'd been reduced to fans and randos on dating apps whenever she traveled to a new location for a film shoot.

Despite the diversity, the men with whom she'd tried to flirt always reacted the same in her presence. Her toothy smiles were met with grimaces. Her attempts at small talk were deflected with grumbles. Flirtatious comments were parried with rude jokes.

This had to end. Somehow.

She'd thought her fortunes would improve when her current director told her he wanted to shoot in the small city where she'd been living before she hit it big. But even here, her luck had remained the same, though so much else had changed.

The deserted side street she now walked was familiar; the storefronts and other establishments she passed were all different. The usual urban churn. She'd expected nothing less after ten years. But the massive structure that loomed ahead was a shock.

She had expected to see the densely wooded park where she'd enjoyed so many walks and talks with her best friend. Instead, the trees in the area were sparse, all of them overshadowed by a multi-sided, red-brick building crowned with a black dome.

Studded with black windows and some wooden doors, the structure looked as if it were more than a century old. As she neared, Deanna counted three sides from her perspective. Assuming all sides were the same length all the way around, she figured the structure would look like an octagon from above.

There was nothing obvious about its design and no signs giving any hints to the building's purpose. Intrigued, she couldn't resist walking the stone pathway leading to a set of mahogany double doors.

Both doors had eye-level square black windows. *Curious* was etched in gold lettering on the left door's glass. *Collections* was etched on the right window.

Figuring there were worse ways to spend a Sunday than exploring, Deanna grasped the right door's iron handle and, with some effort, pulled the heavy door open just enough for her to squeeze inside.

She entered a spacious, semicircular reception area absent any interesting features save for a large rectangular desk. A man and a woman garbed in gray suits stood behind it. Both stared straight ahead, their hands crossed behind their backs. Neither spoke a word. Deanna's attention shifted between them and the arched doorways lining the walls. She counted eight open doorways, dimly lit and evenly spaced.

Her footsteps echoed in the sterile lobby as she approached the desk. The stone-faced man and woman did not look at her. Even after Deanna cleared her throat, neither showed any sign of movement.

She thus jumped a little when the man suddenly said, "Free of charge, ma'am," in a low, rough voice.

The woman languidly lifted her right arm and gestured toward some of the dark doorways. Deanna shuddered as she met the woman's pale gray eyes. Her pupils were mere pinpricks.

Deanna stumbled back a couple of paces before turning and drifting toward the first doorway her eyes landed on. She gave no thought to any of them being much different from the others. They likely led to different areas of the building, but without a map, she had no way of knowing what any of those areas might hold. One was as good as another.

She padded down a dim corridor. Aromas of mildew and wet dog fussed with her nostrils, almost persuading her to turn back. Soon enough, however, the passageway deposited her into a large, hazy room featuring glass or crystalline structures of various shapes, sizes, and hues. Each contained something of interest—exotic plants and flowers, bizarre sculptures, or performance artists. An exhibition of curious items, collected. The building was a museum of some sort.

A small number of other men and women were also here, wending their way through, pausing to linger before the exhibits that grabbed their attention.

As Deanna sauntered in among them, the fusty odors gave way to subtle floral aromas. A pale green haze pervaded the air, which itself seemed to pulse, as if dim lights strobed from unseen directions.

The other people ambled about in pairs or alone, their muffled footsteps no louder than their whispered words. They spanned the range of ages, yet all were garbed in attire as drab as the gloomy outdoors. She regarded the few who passed in close proximity to her.

All were expressionless. Their eyes seemed to be looking

off into the distance. None acknowledged her presence in any way; a few even came close to bumping into her before she slid out of their way. Their slow and low speech sounded no more coherent to her even when she tried concentrating on what was said.

She gave up and devoted her attention to the main attractions. The hazy atmosphere's pulsing rhythms seemed to nudge her from piece to piece to piece. But something within her drew her closer to a distant rectangular object, a silvery screen.

As she neared it, the screen intermittently reflected her mirror image. Once she was within a certain proximity, however, she saw through the glass more clearly.

The exhibit was like a giant fish tank made with double-paned windows that had silvery glitter swimming between the panes. Instead of a fish, the tank held a woman—dancing and singing—seemingly both lost to herself and lost in a joy of her own making. No water, but a flurry of multihued leaves carried by furious gusts swam around her as she whirled about.

Deanna read the artwork's tombstone for a description. It was brief: *Do unto others as they have done unto you.* The artist had an unpronounceable name, but he or she had titled their piece *The Silver Green.* Seemed fitting.

Approximately the same age as Deanna, the singing, barefoot woman was ochre hued, clad in a dark green spaghetti-strap mini dress, and vaguely familiar. Her voice was mature, assured—though, perhaps owing to the glass, Deanna could only hear it when standing within a few paces of the exhibit.

The museum had no guards and no rope encouraging viewers to keep their distance. As a fellow performer, Deanna tried to be respectful. *Do unto others . . .* But the song was like nothing she'd ever heard before, drawing her closer to hear more.

Though as disjointed as many songs tend to be, Deanna

was able to take the visuals and the singer's words and piece them into a narrative.

The woman was lost in a storm . . . had gotten lost on her way to meet her boyfriend—a meeting during which she'd planned to break up with him.

Or she was on her way to a blind date, but she couldn't remember the location.

Or an ex-boyfriend was stalking her with ill intent; everywhere she went, she saw him nearby, but apparently, he didn't remember exactly what she looked like, so he ended up attacking (and getting bested by) women who had only one physical trait in common with her.

Rooted, Deanna may've stood gazing at the spectacle for ten or fifty minutes, gradually realizing the song was about a woman lost in the storm of her own mind and, as a result, lost in time and space. The performer's darkly comical performance was a jazz singer's lost-love ballad twisted with a blues singer's ramble about revenge gone wrong.

Deanna was so enthralled with it all that, when the singer approached the glass in front of her and pushed her arms through the glittering screen as if she were simply extending them through a waterfall, Deanna had no second thoughts about placing her hands into the singer's and squeezing tight as the singer tugged, pulling Deanna inside the tank, into her world.

Passing through the glass, Deanna experienced an onrush of colored melodies, a pleasurable derangement of her senses that eventually smoothed with the caress of crisp, cool breezes. Her vision cleared, revealing that she stood across from the singer, their hands still clasped.

Walls of polychromatic leaves surrounded them on all sides, even above and below. The refreshing breezes caused the leaves to flutter and produce a pleasant susurration, but they didn't move from their place.

Despite no obvious light source, Deanna could see well around her. The smiling singer appeared much as she had on the other side of the glass, though Deanna hadn't noticed the black lipstick before.

Haze also pervaded the air here, making the singer slightly indistinct in Deanna's eyes, despite their nearness. With one exception. The artist's unblinking eyes were sharp and distinct. The irises were more orange than hazel, their shape more octagonal than round. *Contacts*, Deanna figured. *Exotics for an exotic artist.* But they couldn't divert the sense of familiarity she felt with this woman.

"Who are you?" Deanna's throat constricted as she spoke, making her words sound strangled.

"I am the woman who possesses this installation." The singer spoke in a quiet voice.

"I mean"—Deanna paused, cleared her throat—"do you have a name?"

"Not at the moment."

A performer who is at one with the piece, Deanna figured. Like an actor in a movie has whatever designation the script gives her, whether it's a name, an occupation, or just a type. While the singer was here, she was inseparable from *The Silver Green*.

Deanna felt the singer's hands moistening.

"When you were viewing me just now," the singer said, "something troubled you. That's the intended effect on the viewer. You saw something that connected with you, deep inside. You've come here, come to me for a reason."

Deanna smiled awkwardly, trying to hide her discomfort at the sweating hands. "I guess I just connected with a fellow artist." She tried to gently pull from the singer's grasp.

"I guess you did. I can also guess you're having some trouble in your life, trouble connecting with a significant other."

The singer's hands dropped steeply in temperature.

Deanna tried with more effort to break the grasp. The singer didn't flinch. Beyond her moving lips and her hair stirring in the breeze, she didn't move. She had yet to even blink.

"Let me tell you my story," the singer said. "The story of a foolish young woman. A trusting woman . . ."

Deanna's teeth clenched as the cold traveled from her hands to her arms.

"In my early twenties, I had my heart set on being an actor. My best friend did as well. But we had different tastes, strong preferences for the types of roles we'd accept. Moreover, we promised we'd never audition for a part the other wanted.

"One day, my friend accompanied me to an audition for an outré movie. A dark, romantic thriller about an avant-garde nightclub singer. It wasn't my friend's sort of thing at all. She'd just come for moral support. I did well at the audition—or thought I did until I heard the joke: my friend got the callback. My friend who didn't even audition."

Deanna shivered. What had felt like the caresses of spring breezes now felt like the fingers of late autumn scratching at her skin.

"We took a walk in a park like we often did to relax. The express purpose on this occasion was to talk about what had happened. The talk turned into an argument. Soon we were fighting with more than just words. My friend got the best of me. She later got the part."

Deanna tried to talk, but her chattering teeth prevented coherency.

"It was originally a romantic thriller. Working title: *Alluring*. Once my friend stole the part, they rewrote the film to suit her. Turned it into a romantic comedy, released in some markets as *Coy Pond*. It was my ex-friend's breakout role. The beginning of the backstabber's career."

Freezing, Deanna's body trembled violently as she fought with all her strength to pull away. She kicked at the woman, but her feet only passed through air. She tried spitting at her, but her throat was too dry. Fear commingled with frustration made her eyes water.

"You never tried to help me. You knocked me out and left me, bloody, in the park, not caring what happened. Two addicts came along shortly after and . . . Well, they finished your job. You left me for dead. This is how I ended up."

Crying and shrieking, Deanna stamped her feet. She'd given up trying to shake free from the woman's grip; their hands were connected as if to the same body. All she had left was pleading. "Let me *go*! It's not my fault! It's *not* my fault! It's not my fault you're—"

"A composition of tiny crystals—that's what I've been reduced to. Interdimensional particulates . . . Thanks to you."

"*No!*"

"Stay still and *look* at me."

A sensation of warmth pulsed through Deanna, stilling her, if not calming her. Light headed, she felt ready to pass out but knew that would not be allowed. She could only heave as she gazed at the artful work—the soul of her one-time best friend.

"You're responsible for the expiration of my flesh, my giving up the ghost. In the process, you forfeited your own soul. You have known this, felt this for the past ten years, though you could never bring yourself to admit it. You could never stoop to be honest, even to yourself. You'll never have a soulmate—because you have no soul. Mine, however, proved to be quite tenacious."

Deanna shook her head. "I . . . I'm sorry. So sorry. I don't want to die. Please . . ." She looked about her, searching for any sign of hope among the walls of multicolored leaves.

The singer nodded. "You can leave. But there is only one way out." The singer slowly released her grip.

Deanna remained where she stood, trembling.

"You've been soulless for some time now. Your only way to reenter the world of the living is to reacquire a soul."

"How?" Deanna stuttered.

"Ask forgiveness for your crime."

"God . . . *please*—"

"Not to God. Ask forgiveness of *me*."

Deanna looked at the singer's eyes, still the most distinct aspect of her. She thought she understood now. She focused her gaze, looked deep within—deep enough to reach and latch on to what had made them best friends all those years ago—and then spoke.

"Please. Please forgive me. I'm so sorry. Please let me return to my life."

The singer beamed at her. "You have your forgiveness. Now, let us embrace. Like long-lost friends."

The leaves' susurration grew to screams as the colorful foliage swarmed them both, cutting and slicing only one of them.

FRESH COFFEE in hand from the upscale and new-to-her café, Mathilda strolled gracefully down the sidewalk, flashing a broad smile to all who passed her, even greeting a few with a wink. What was not to be happy about? The sun was bright in the sky, and it was the last day of shooting in the town where she'd gotten her start.

She'd be leaving a lot of memories behind. *Buried,* where they belonged.

With her new attitude, not to mention a new body, she thought a new name was fitting. It surprised her director, but he said they'd deal with the press and publicity matters later. There was a movie to finish.

And there was a new direction for her to begin. With all the acclaim and success this body had gathered in romantic comedies, she thought it high time she got back to her original passion: darker films, the twisted and the outré. Maybe she'd even drop acting and start directing.

She cast a glance across the street. Where there'd once been a densely wooded park she'd often frequented with a former friend, there now was a symbolic cemetery.

Several years ago, a business developer had all the trees cleared for a venture that never got off the ground. A local artist purchased the land, intending to revitalize it while also turning it into an impermanent art project. He'd invited ordinary citizens to participate.

The artist had planted several trees but had also set down a good number of temporary tombstones. The silvery, octagonal objects were oriented in such a way as to reflect the leaves of the growing trees. If one ventured close enough to any one of the artworks, they'd see the gold etchings that told the brief stories of random people who used to walk through the park enjoying nature, enjoying the companionship of family and friends, enjoying contemplation.

An impermanent cemetery for a bunch of nobodies' dead dreams.

Mathilda smiled to herself as she continued on to her hotel. For the time being, the cemetery's green would suffice to be alluring to the soulless, poisonous to those who reject repentance.

THE DUMPS

In a mirror's clear error . . .

Hendrick didn't remember where he'd first come across the phrase. He could've read or heard it any number of places over the past four decades. But whenever or wherever its origin, it came to him often these days. He didn't even need to stand in front of a clear mirror. A bakery's street window would do.

The faint outline of a gourd—a misshapen man but perfect butternut squash—stood directly across from him. The sight depressed him, slumped his shoulders maybe an inch lower, but didn't deter. It took little energy and no trickery to see beyond his own washed-out image to focus on the sweets. The decadent desirables.

He'd swing back for a late breakfast. Hell, he likely would've done so even if he hadn't stopped.

He could've kept walking, chin lowered, eyes on the cracked, uneven sidewalk, watching his step as he made his way to his therapy appointment on this dreary Saturday morning. He would've liked to think the aromas lifted his chin, made him halt, turn his head, and stare at the pastries. But who was he kidding?

He'd traveled this route often. He could find the bakery's location in his sleep. He, in fact, often did dream of devouring the forbidden foods. He just as often woke up damp with sweat, heaving as he tried to regain his breath.

Presently, the donuts before his eyes—a long john with vanilla icing; chocolate and cinnamon, twisting into a tiger tail; a flattened sphere, gushing raspberry jam out of a perfect slit; an otherwise bare donut with random dollops of marshmallow; a chocolate cake ring with a plug of peanut butter frosting, spiraling upward into a cone, filling the pastry's hole—the sight of them, the consideration of them, stirred a number of different yet related pangs within him, complementing hungers.

A drop of liquid burst on his forehead, followed by another on his cheek. Though the forecast called for a bright and sunny spring day, dawn had yawned a gray sky. Now the drizzle that the thick, dark clouds had promised had finally come.

He'd known the release was inevitable, but he'd neglected to grab an umbrella before leaving his house, or a jacket with a hood. His boots were sturdy and water resistant. But his jeans and long-sleeve shirt were both relatively fashionable. He'd rather not have them stained with rainwater at the beginning of a long day.

He turned away from the display and hurried down the sidewalk, futilely attempting to evade the thick, viscid droplets that splattered on him with increasing frequency.

After lumbering down sidewalks light on pedestrians for two and a half blocks, he paused under the awning of a building across the street from his destination. He needed to catch his breath.

Checking over his skin and clothes, he determined he

wasn't too damp. His face and forearms, however, were slightly sticky. On his fingertips, he saw a thin, oily film displaying half of a rainbow's colors.

Like lightning, thoughts flashed across his consciousness, linked with images: in-the-grind workers whose labor was never truly appreciated by any except Heaven, which rained down the oil that would slick and stick people into the firm understanding that blue-collar workers had an in with the Man beyond the blue sky. The blue collars weren't the stewards of the Earth. Quite the opposite. They were the hidden princes. And when the Day of Reckoning came, those who'd abused such workers with their words and attitudes would be brushed to the sewers.

He again rubbed his fingers across his forearms and cheeks. They felt like any would against plain-water-slicked skin. Upon examination, the rainbow sheen was gone.

Maybe his retributive fantasies were getting the better of him today. Either way, he thanked the heavens an in-house shower was required before his therapy session.

Still feeling the effects of his clumsy run, he tried to steady his breath—taking deeper inhales, releasing slower exhales—as he gazed at the broad, multistoried building across the street.

A bulky, drab structure, it attracted no sightseers. Like a brutalist government building, it drew only the attention and bodies of those who needed to come, those who had a problem that needed solving if they were to go on yet another day, those who had deep wounds that needed a special kind of salve. At least, that's how the black marketeers had pitched the services of those who worked on the premises.

Over the past couple of years, Hendrick had found himself intrigued when he heard rumors via the grapevine of electricians, HVAC technicians, carpenters, and project managers with whom he sometimes worked. Older folks passing on their own blue secrets for rejuvenation.

He'd caught enough of his breath to keep it under control as he hurried across the street. Traffic wasn't a concern. It was practically nonexistent, as was normal during his Saturday morning visits. There were no residences on this street, and most establishments didn't open until later in the day. Anyplace anyone needed to go could be reached by more efficient routes.

He ascended the steps to the covered porch and tried, in vain, to peer through the double door's windows. It was like trying to look through drywall. He turned to the call box on his left and punched in this week's eight-digit code. Upon hearing the buzz, he pulled open one of the doors.

After traversing an empty foyer that contained nothing but cobwebs, dingy walls, and a weathered chessboard floor, he pushed through another set of creaking double doors to enter a broad anteroom, a teal octagon with a nine-color checkerboard floor and many doors, some of them leading to passageways, others leading to nooks harboring stairways or elevators.

Many doors, but no paintings, pictures, or decorations of any kind on the floor or walls, absences that weren't surprising, considering the building's exterior. But there were also no directories or guides, no welcome desk or even a welcome sign. Before entering the building, a visitor had to not only settle on his service but also know the correct pathway for reaching the appropriate reception area.

A few other men and two or three women populated the spacious area, but none spoke or made eye contact with anyone else. Each was finding his or her own way, silently and—at their own relative pace—with haste.

Hendrick wasn't in much of a rush. He was early for his appointment. And his breath was still a little heavy. When he reached his suite, he didn't want to greet his receptionist panting like a dog.

Instead, he took some time to count the doors—the exits—from the anteroom. As his breath steadied, he raised his gaze upward to the faded and damaged mural on the ceiling. Enough of it remained intact for a viewer to make out the numerous men and women garbed in white outfits, ranging from gleaming robes to doctor and nurse outfits. A clear implication of medical professionals sharing the work of holy men and women—*angels*, even.

He was in the one-time lobby of a facility known as the Haracomb, known now to those who were privy as the Warren, though there was nothing indoors or outdoors to denote the name, let alone the services provided. The existence of the therapeutic spa, however, was no secret. Anyone looking knew how to find it. Whether they were allowed entry was another matter.

Euphoric and curious after his first visit, Hendrick had done extensive research on the place.

Haracomb was a not-too-clever combination of *hair* and *comb. Hair is on top of the body, and one must maintain it.* The originators' idea was to play against the term *catacomb*—an underground burial chamber—as the building was devised to be a medical facility, one constructed at the behest of aging rich folks, affluent men and women who had no loved ones left in their lives but wanted to be cared for and looked after in their old age, in comfort and privacy, by professionals they could trust.

The original intention had been to give each dying resident a large, private studio apartment, one lavishly decorated and generously supplied with whatever they demanded for comfort. Trusted, handpicked medical professionals and caregivers were to be on-site at all times; some of them even had their own living compartments. They were expected to respond to the needs and emergencies of the elderly at a moment's notice.

A circle of wealthy old friends formed a pact and initiated the project, funding it and occupying it. As the sickest and oldest of them began to pass away, the remaining occupants invited younger acquaintances—all wealthy, all of appropriate social standing—to take up residence in the building when they reached the appropriate age for entry. The cycle continued for just over two decades before the dream, the concept itself, began to die.

Invitees increasingly rejected the idea of the original pact. Most of the elderly, debilitated folks in the metropolitan area who had the option of living in the Haracomb preferred the company of their families or to just die alone. The paucity of aging men and women who had the wealth, vision, and desire to buy into the founders' original dream ensured the project had only short-lived success.

The property was eventually bought, renovated, and repurposed by an entrepreneur who was as wealthy as he or she was reclusive. Perhaps taking some sort of perverse delight in the idea *Haracomb* was supposed to be the obverse of *catacomb*, he or she took the word apart, refocused on *hair*, then *hare*, and then came up with the Warren.

Presently, Hendrick passed through one of the lobby's many doors and walked a short distance to an elevator. Two others stood nearby, waiting. A lean man in his forties with a drastically receding hairline and a short, bowlegged man in his late fifties or early sixties. The latter's hands were stuffed into his pants pockets. The lean man crossed his hands behind his back.

Hendrick wondered if they were here for the same service as he but wouldn't dare ask. Neither man said a word to him either. Both, however, tossed at least one glance his way. It was easy to ignore others in the lobby, but one wanted to size up—even briefly—anyone with whom they'd be sharing an elevator car.

When the elevator door slid open, the short man got on first, followed at a respectable distance by the taller. Hendrick pushed the button for a floor two levels lower than their destinations and stared straight ahead as the car ascended.

The elevator's door wasn't reflective. He couldn't see what either man was doing behind him. But he could hear them. One clicked his teeth repeatedly—a slow-motion chatter. The other breathed loudly, at an increasing rate. Both were getting more excited as they came closer to their respective destinations, their preferred therapies. He'd wager at least one of them had sweaty palms.

Hendrick wished they exhibited a bit more poise. Maybe they were wishing their therapies—whatever they were—went beyond the boundaries to which they'd initially agreed. Maybe they were hoping that, today, they'd make whatever they were fantasizing about a reality.

He entertained the thought that he was in a car with two deviants—two men who wanted to go to sexual extremes but didn't have the means or the courage to do so. They fantasized about it, were possibly doing so now, but their therapies were intended to take them only so far in the sensual journey in order to release the tension—only temporarily, of course. Maybe they were frequent visitors.

Or maybe his imagination was running, taking him away from the thought that he might be more like them than different.

He wasn't embarrassed about needing therapy. He wasn't even embarrassed for the men—whatever therapies they might be getting or for whatever reason. At least they were getting help for their conditions, whatever they might be. But he also hoped they weren't embarrassed or too anxious. Nervous anticipation, premature excitement—none of it was helpful. He knew well from experience.

Hendrick was about to open his mouth, say a few words—maybe some aphorism he'd once heard—to calm or reassure the men. But the car stopped. He'd reached his floor.

He proceeded down a dimly lit corridor for two or three dozen paces, then turned a corner, passing no one as he made his way to the cream-colored door. Office 708. Jasmine incense met his nostrils the moment he entered.

He maneuvered between the reception area's potted plants, sparse empty chairs, and lone empty couch, making his way to the check-in desk. Two women sat behind it; one stood in front. Bethania, Claire, and Cecelia. All wore gray clean-room frocks.

The three paused their conversation to greet him with wincing eyes, equally tight smiles, and a slight bow of their heads.

No words. No need.

They knew him, and he knew the procedure. Claire, the standing woman, turned a shoulder—a cue for him to follow her down a hallway.

He was always on time for his appointments, but each time —during the walk—part of him felt he wasn't supposed to be here. Today was no different. Such treatment that was in store, he didn't deserve. It was a ridiculous feeling to have, especially considering how he'd just felt in the elevator. Not to mention how many times he'd gone through the therapy before.

He also wondered whether his presence signified any kind of progress. For the longest time in his adulthood, early Saturday mornings were reserved for sunrise exercise and big-breakfast rewards. Two routines, one canceling out the other. He'd repeatedly cursed the habitual cycle but couldn't renounce it, not until therapy took its place. But as blissful as the sessions were, the fundamental problem remained.

Claire escorted him through gossamer-like veils that partitioned a snaking corridor until they stopped in front of his rented suite, the entry and exit point of which was a private bathroom, a room of pale gray walls, white fixtures, and vividly colorful bottles and tubes.

He didn't know for sure, but over his repeated visits, he'd come to figure office 708 contained at least six private suites, maybe eight, each of which could likely host sessions of up to four clients a day, accounting for the time it would take to clean up after each appointment.

He intentionally hadn't showered since Friday afternoon. What would be the point when the rules required each client to rinse on the premises prior to each session? Besides, he took some comfort in arriving to these appointments soiled with dried sweat and dead skin cells—vestiges of his feverish dreams and the frustrating life that fed them. Good reminders that his sorry self truly needed help, the sort of help that only his cuddle bunny could provide, even if the effects were only temporary.

Claire left him as she'd greeted him—silently and with a smile. There was no need for instructions on what to do. It would've been a waste of breath to ask if he had any questions. After three months of weekly visits, he was more than familiar with the routine.

Careful to not so much as glance at any of the room's mirrors, he stripped slowly, taking care to hang or fold each article of clothing as soon as it was off his body.

Before stepping into the shower, he examined the array of hair-and-body wash containers. The spa's own signature brand. He quickly narrowed his choice between the clary sage and the fragrance-free. The former was touted as an aid to relax the nervous—the first- and second-timers. The latter was for more experienced clients.

He gripped the clary sage tube but only to open it and inhale its aromas. He wasn't nervous, he told himself. He couldn't be, shouldn't be, after his twelve prior visits. He just liked to pause every now and then to take in the scents of flowers and herbs, let their aromas swim with his senses and bring his mind back to more innocent, guiltlessly pleasurable days, when he could easily resist unhealthy temptations.

In the shower, he waited for the water to reach a lukewarm temperature, then doused his hair and skin before squirting the fragrance-free foam into his hand. He lathered from head to toe —circular strokes over his abdomen and chest; long, sweeping strokes over his arms and legs—washing off the accumulations from dreams and morning weather. He used similar motions outside the shower, employing both towel and hair dryer to eliminate every damp area.

After sliding into his boxer briefs, he opened the door opposite the one by which he'd entered.

Warm air from ceiling vents caressed his skin as he padded down the dark, carpeted passageway toward the glowing room at its end. The room's sliding door had been pulled all the way open; the entrance was flush with a magenta luminescence sourced from somewhere within. He'd the impression he was approaching a portal to another world.

Crossing the threshold, he didn't find himself in lush or exotic surroundings, but the atmosphere of the five-walled room, bare of everything but essentials, gave him the sense of a realm wholly separate from his day-to-day.

A ceiling fan lamp hung high over the large circular mattress at the room's center. The dimmed light bulbs tended pink. The walls, lavender. The colors combined to lend an exotic hue to the skin of Klavdiya, the nearly naked woman reclining on her side in the center of the mattress.

He smiled as his eyes met hers, but he didn't let them rest there. Hourglass shaped, she wore only a bra and panties, both sheer. Any extra pounds her body carried were put to good use in the squeezable and lovable areas. Having never seen her outside the room, he wondered how her short, spiky hair appeared in natural light. Her hair color, her skin color—both mysteries. Irrelevant ones, as she was open to him in a way that was far more important.

Pillows of varying lengths and shapes surrounded her. Sometimes they used one or two during a session; other times the support provided by her—her body—was more than enough. As the door slid shut behind him, he wondered how this session would go.

Ambient music piped in from some device or speaker out of view, providing the room's predominant noise. Neither he nor Klavdiya said a thing as he slowly inched forward. It was their well-established protocol to let the room's light and music immerse them before first words were spoken.

He stood at the edge of the mattress—gazing, assessing—as the room's atmosphere had its way with him. After a moment, his eyes or perhaps something about his posture signaled to her that he was ready.

"Welcome." She spoke softly, with a slight accent. Eastern European, he'd always thought. Possibly Russian. Maybe Ukrainian. All wild guesses. He could've been way off.

Wherever she was from, she was here now, in front of him. Inviting. Promising.

He bowed his head—"Thank you for welcoming me"—and kneeled before her, lowering himself gently onto the mattress. With care, he crawled toward her.

When within a certain proximity, both shifted their positions, coming up to their knees to warmly embrace.

Once disengaged, Hendrick turned his back to her as he settled into a sitting position. Knees up, feet and buttocks flat. Klavdiya whispered into his right ear.

"Relax and release."

Hendrick leaned backward, allowing her arms to snake over his shoulders. He closed his eyes as she cradled his head with her chin, arms, and bosom.

"Now . . . state your purpose and *breathe*."

"I want . . . *reclamation* . . ." He drew out the last word, extending it to a prolonged exhale. After a pause, he inhaled just as deeply.

He maintained his own breathing pattern for only two cycles. His head cradled, his bare neck and upper back pressed flat against her soft but supportive midsection, he couldn't help but fall in gently with her pattern as her chest rose and fell with inhalations and exhalations.

Their session had begun.

A session of physical touch—cuddle therapy—authentic connection . . . Touted as a more intimate method than most of destressing, instilling internal calm. The therapy comforted him, put him more in tune with himself, alleviated the anger he usually felt. *Reclamation* . . . To no longer feel sorry—depressed —about his sorry self.

When he was with Klavdiya, he was at peace with the fact that he was among the bottom-feeders. She made him feel content, sometimes even elated, to keep on living as he was.

Both a reminder and a respite, Klavdiya was something of a charging station for him, evidenced by how his nerves hummed when in her embrace. Such a delight to be held and catered to by a beautiful woman rather than the dogs he normally attracted. The jump-offs. The pickup-and-dumps.

Rearranging their positions, he laid his head on her lap; she played with his hair.

Soon they eased to a reverse twist: he lay on his back, his legs slightly open; face up, she positioned herself in between his legs and on top of him, her head resting on his chest.

Eventually they moved on to spooning. Despite being heavier, Hendrick acted as the little spoon. Lying on their sides, Klavdiya's arms wrapped around his, her stomach pressed against his back, her breasts against his neck.

Without words and with only a few guttural sounds, they maintained this position for uncounted minutes until her voice drifted to him, sounding as if it were spoken from inside his head.

"You've been seeing me for a few months now, and we've mostly existed in silence. But I feel I'm not really helping you get to the root of your issue."

Despite their tender delivery, her words were as jarring as they were perplexing.

The cuddle bunnies offered a unique version of cuddle therapy. They went a little further than the mainstream cuddle therapists, who all had a strict clothes-on policy. They catered to a specific clientele, a more exclusive and trustworthy clientele that preferred more skin-to-skin contact. Hendrick didn't think himself a fool; he knew from day one these women were just a step or two removed from escorts. And he'd figured all they really cared about was repeat business—from their "respectful" customers, that is. He never dreamed any of them would actually want to hear about what ailed their customers, let alone try to heal them.

"Umm," he began. Lingering confusion left him at a loss for what to say. He swallowed, then tried again—but words continued to fail.

"It's all right," she continued in her soft voice. "You can be open here—*free* yourself. It's what we invite clients to do. At their own comfort level. In the unusual cases of prolonged silence, after twelve weeks, we like to give our clients a little nudge. Often, that's all they need to open up."

"I . . . I wouldn't know where to begin."

"I do. I've been trained to know." She chuckled quietly at some joke or witticism that eluded him. "You are . . . a one-time athlete . . . or a one-time artist . . . or some other one-time figure adored by the opposite sex, and you feel you've lost your touch. So you've come here to feel the touch of the beautiful, the accepting, the comforting. You want to regain what you believe you've lost—but you believe it's impossible."

The woman had been trained well, he thought.

"Let's talk about when you were happiest. And the most miserable. I sense it was the same period of time for you."

"I . . . I *was* an athlete. A wrestler. In high school. Trade school. Constantly trying to keep my weight, stay in my preferred weight class. A lot of dieting. A lot of exercise. A lot of running with the trash-bag armor."

"Your body wanted to be of a certain shape, but you were forcing it into another. Your *preference*."

"No. I mean, anyone who wants to be an athlete has to get their body under control. Get it and keep it strong, resilient, healthy."

"Healthy body, healthy mind."

"That's right."

"Unless the body only appears healthy but is unhappy. In which case, the body may try to communicate with the mind, and vice versa. Discreet communications with the subconscious. As subtle yet powerful as the sun's communication with plants."

"Do, uh, the plants communicate back? With the sun?"

"They communicate with us."

He didn't quite get the analogy. Something about it seemed off, as if she were translating a saying that made more sense in her native tongue. But the idea of plants and communication got him thinking.

"I was big on vegetables when I was in my prime. Not a vegetarian, but . . . Well, anyway, one day, in my early twenties, I found that most of them repulsed me. I continued to eat them, out of duty, duty to my body, but the portions diminished as I got older."

"What made you want to become an athlete in the first place?"

"Action figures . . . comic books . . ." He chuckled. "I guess I was highly suggestable as a kid. I saw these toys and cartoons and thought it would be nice to look like that. I wanted a body like that, and I wanted to compete. So I worked at it, got what I wanted. Athletic success. Success with women. Yeah, I liked the adoration I got, from all corners. But I had to put those days behind me when I became a plumber full time. The rat race—a different type of competition. There, to be competitive, to get ahead and stay ahead, different abilities are required from what's useful in the gym or on the mat, and I worked on honing those. I did well, but my appetite started changing. I had less and less success with the women. With the women I wanted. But I was doing well on the job. Still do well. Very well. But my body has gone to pot."

"Is that what you see when you look at yourself? A pot?"

"I don't look at myself. Not for any sustained amount of time. I don't need to study my body. I know how I am. I'm in a fat person's profession. I *feel* how I am. I don't have the energy I had twenty or even five years ago at thirty-seven. I probably talk like a fat person. I certainly walk like one."

"You could alter your posture, walk a different way. Like models are taught."

He chuckled again. "I ain't no model. Besides, I've tried. It's uncomfortable. That's what I'm saying—anything I do with diet, exercise, to try to change myself is *painful*. Or makes me nauseous. Or both. I crave sweets now, like I did when I was a young kid, and I indulge."

"Hmm."

His body vibrated subtly with her hum.

"Mirrors . . ."

She seemed to have begun a thought out loud. Hendrick was content to let her finish it unspoken. But after a moment, she continued.

"You avoid them as much as possible. Instead, you find the image of yourself in others. How you think they see you."

"I *know* how they see me. I know how I am. Fat. I don't date anymore. I *can't*. I just pick up—" He paused, cleared his throat. "Well . . . I don't have a meaningful social life. And I *do* see myself in the reflections of glass—it's unavoidable. Windows. Display cases . . ."

"Hmm."

He again seemed to vibrate from deep within, as if his bone marrow were unstable.

"Have you ever considered that your actual appearance has nothing to do with anything? That there are deeper issues?"

"You going to tell me to see a real psychiatrist now?" He regretted the words the moment they left his lips. "I mean—I *didn't* mean—"

Her laugh, louder than any vocal utterance he'd ever heard her make, not only cut him off but seemed to dust his bones with ice crystals—formations that melted quickly as his body shivered. She held him tighter.

"I'm not about to send you to anyone else. But I would like to inform you, one of my best and sweetest clients, that we offer many different levels of service here. Some are pricier than others, but they are very effective."

The upsell. He knew it would come someday.

The basic cuddling service for which he was paying was far more expensive than any similar service in the city, so an increase for a premium service was expected. A six-figure-earning bachelor with no ex and no kids, he could likely afford it. But he didn't like to toss money to the wind. "How effective?"

"Words can't convey. You'll only know once you try it."

A minute or two of silence passed between them. Over the months, he'd come to trust this woman. Aside from money, what had he to lose? Likely the extra money would just go to satisfying his gut anyway.

"Okay. What do I need to do?"

She kissed the top of his head, then readjusted her position until they were face to face, hugging. "I'll need you to bury your head . . ."

He followed her commands as they engaged in a sensuous dance, noncompetitive wrestling, losing their garments and shifting through various positions while their skin rubbed, their lips pressed, and their heart rates increased.

She gave him no warnings as she spat and licked, pinched and smacked, kneaded and scratched. He was in her thrall, willing to go along, obey, even as her body—in its maneuvers— seemed to bend, twist, and coil in improbable ways.

When he thought his tongue and lips might go dry from overuse, sweet aromas found his nostrils, causing him to salivate.

Klavdiya . . . Her scent was redolent of vanilla and strawberries—but he knew this was just his imagination, a hint of a submerged desire rising to prominence. Klavdiya and, he presumed, the other cuddle bunnies had a policy of rinsing themselves clean of all fragrances—perfumes, lotions, shampoos —so as not to overwhelm any client who might be sensitive enough to have an allergic reaction.

But the aromas grew stronger. And he was certainly having a reaction, reimagining the pastries he'd seen earlier. *A perfect slit . . . Sweetness gushing . . .*

With a series of shudders, he lost himself. His vision blurred, blanked out. When he recovered, panting, he was lying on top of Klavdiya. They were tightly embraced—nose to nose, eye to eye. Their skin, viscid.

He wasn't hungry anymore—certainly not for sweets. He'd gotten his fill.

Still panting, he forced out his question. "So . . . how much more . . . expensive . . . was that?"

"The price . . . yes. Let's discuss that next time."

EYES DOWNCAST, Hendrick removed his tenacious boxer shorts and stepped into the shower.

What had he agreed to? What had Klavdiya done to him? He chuckled at the thought that perhaps she'd recorded whatever she'd done and would later use the video to blackmail or otherwise publicly humiliate him, ruin his business. If that idea had been in her head, why wait thirteen weeks?

The questions kept coming even after he shut off the water. Preoccupied with sorting through possible answers as he dried off, he didn't realize his eyes had drifted to the mirror until he was staring dead-on at a reflection of his naked body.

His belly protruded; his pectorals were not as defined as he would have preferred, but he wasn't all that bad—certainly not as bad as he'd assumed. There was noticeable muscle tone in his arms and chest. His thighs had some definition as well. And his skin lacked any signs of the scratches and bites Klavdiya had inflicted.

As the glass held his gaze, he felt his spine lengthen, his shoulders broaden. His stomach did not shrink into a six-pack but flattened enough so that his chest—just barely—stuck out farther than it.

An uncertain smile spread across his face. Pieces of memories strobed in his mind. The first few times he'd had sex . . .

After each time, he felt more like a man. Each time, he spent the next few hours and sometimes the following days walking taller, strutting confidently, talking easily to friends, haters, and strangers alike. *Blissed* out of his mind. When the feeling went away, he went to find more of what had put him in that state.

The pretty girls he attracted thanks to his athletic prowess —over the course of his school years, they came easier and easier—and the subsequent feelings of bliss diminished until they eventually went away altogether. Once he was done with school and began to devote himself to a career, his interest in fooling around had waned. For a number of years, it stayed that way. He'd worked hard to get to where he was now.

But now . . .

Now that he wanted to settle down with the right woman, the sort of woman he rightly deserved, he had no luck. He could get sex—no problem—so long as he was willing to settle for the bottom-feeders. The dumpster chicks. And settle he often did. Why not, when they approached him, and they both had the urge?

But he'd a deeper urge to settle down—and he just couldn't pull the women he truly wanted. It didn't matter that he made six figures, owned his own company. He was still just a plumber in the eyes of many. A toilet plunger. A dirty-pipe cleaner. Once his profession became known to a potential part-

ner, he became an unknown. The romantic partners he desired
. . . They didn't just look down at him; they looked around him,
pinched their noses at him, squinted and spat "phew" at him,
threatened to throw drinks in his face (and sometimes followed
through) before ordering him to dismiss himself or to go and
clean up in a faraway bathroom.

He loved his job. Was successful and made very good
money. But what he did for a living disgusted the objects of his
original desire, the sorts of women he adored and pined after.
The women he chased, they ran or stood their ground and
attacked. None stopped to examine, none took the time to use
their words to excavate, engage him in a conversation so that
they might seek and find the real him.

Gazing at himself in the mirror now, he felt that maybe it
was time to try again.

But first things first. It was Saturday. He had errands
to run.

THE RAIN HAD STOPPED by the time he left the Warren.
The midday air was humid.

Though invigorated with a new sense of self, he walked
slowly down the sidewalks, enthralled by the sight of the pave-
ment giving up its vaporous ghosts. He knew it was just rainwater, but he was inclined to think of death and rebirth. Growth
from up out of the dumps. Something sprouting and reaching
upward from the dirt.

Summer days, numerous ways to play. Add them all up,
enjoy what goes down . . .

A saying from his youth. A saying long forgotten until
today. Was his subconscious trying to tell him something about
the remaining days of spring?

Crossing streets and turning corners, he trod increasingly crowded sidewalks as he made his way to his truck. He tried to keep his focus forward, but his peripheral vision was sharp, alert to happenings on either side of him.

Steps away from passing in front of a hair salon, he noted someone approaching the door from the inside. He paused, letting the statuesque brunette with the French bob exit the shop and walk in front of him. He continued on, unable to keep his eyes off her legs, her hips, her feline grace. The boutique was high end; the woman's clothes, tasteful. He wondered what she did for a living. Real estate lawyer, maybe?

Perhaps sensing that he was devoting the bulk of his attention to her or that she was possibly being followed, the woman cast a look at him over her shoulder. Hendrick expected her to either speed up or stop and deliver a warning about the mace she carried in her purse.

He slowed his pace, but the woman kept hers. She cast another look over her shoulder and smiled. "Good afternoon."

Hendrick stuttered as he returned the greeting.

The woman tossed another smile his way, then turned a corner and proceeded down a cross street. "Enjoy the day!"

If only he were going her way. He'd maybe catch up to her and start a conversation. But he'd kept walking, and by the time he thought of it, they were at least two blocks apart. She was long out of sight.

Maybe she'd been toying with him anyway. Or maybe she was married, or otherwise spoken for, and just being friendly because she was happy to have her hair done and not have it ruined by rainwater. He'd never know.

He reached his pickup and went on with his errands. Grocery store. Hardware store. Later-than-usual lunch at his favorite burger-and-beer joint. All of it interspersed with communications with employees handling emergency calls.

He was busy, but not so much that he didn't notice attention from the sort of women who used to pass him as if he were a ghost or a ghoul. Pretty women in nice outfits doing double takes and smiling when catching his eye. They were all okay, but they weren't quite at the level of the women he really wanted, the sort of women that he really deserved. No—he'd find those women elsewhere. Places that, lately, he had feared to tread.

Though the fear no longer sat as heavy with him as it had in recent years. He felt lighter. Felt that he could now see—and understand—things more clearly.

When he was a much younger man (or, more accurately, an older kid), it was all intuitive. He needed to get himself into a position—physically and socially—so that women would be willing to pleasure him. As a young, buff wrestler, he was in such a position, and he was skilled enough to accept the women who threw themselves at him and twist and turn them into all sorts of positions that would please both him and them.

He'd gotten away from himself. But this Saturday, he was returning to himself. Klavdiya—his cuddle bunny . . . Whatever she'd done was working like magic.

He added to his list some last-minute errands for the day: shopping for new clothes and shopping for new grounds. If he wanted to play at a higher level, he needed the right gear. And he needed to be seen showing it off in the right spots.

HENDRICK'S DAYTIME experience inspired him to gamble with his Saturday evening. Dressed to the nines in a modish yet somewhat conservative suit, he ventured out to hit scenes he'd never entered before.

Forget the bars beloved by locals. He'd hit up the bars in

the downtown hotels, those frequented by business travelers. Where better to test himself? If he struck out with a woman, it was highly unlikely he'd ever see her again; she'd be off to another city.

True, locals frequented the upper-scale hotel bars as well, but it would be easy to weed them out. The way they spoke, the way they dressed, the fact that they congregated in packs of other locals . . .

Many of the business travelers congregated as well. Fine. He hadn't the skills to separate them out from their associates, and he wouldn't want to risk ire by trying to pick up a woman in the middle of a business deal. He'd zero in on the lonely lovelies.

At the first hotel—and the second—and the third—he made his way slowly to the bar, nonchalantly scanning the entire area while remaining most attentive to those seated at or standing near it. Once he'd sized up an ideal candidate, rather than invading her space by walking right by her or standing next to her, he kept a respectable distance but positioned himself in her line of vision as he ordered his drink. Sometimes he caught her eye. Oftentimes, he didn't. Women on their own were often preoccupied with their phones, taking breaks only to order another drink or fend off pretty boys and Casanovas of the wrong scent or song.

Hendrick used his smile like a concealed weapon, revealing it only to choice targets, those who—if they reciprocated—showed they were open, willing and able to be taken down by him—taken away by him—so that he might assess them with more than just his eyes and judge whether they were truly the one for him.

There were handfuls of women at the first few hotels who piqued his interest, and he managed to strike up conversations with a good percentage of them. But when he could see the chatter was going nowhere, he cut it short.

He promised himself he'd only try one more bar before calling it quits, fully expecting to be home and in bed—alone— by midnight. But the moment he walked into the fourth bar, he'd a sense his luck was about to change.

The wood paneling, leather chairs, and abundance of scotch gave him the immediate impression of entering an old-school gentlemen's club—but the number of classy women wiped the impression away as quickly as it came.

As he made his way to the bar—maneuvering around occu-pied chairs arranged around small round tables and almost fully occupied stools arranged around taller round tables—he appreciated the soft classical music, courtesy of a live pianist. It wasn't the sort of music he'd ever choose to listen to on his own, but it put him in a mood, made him feel as if this were his first stop for the night rather than the last. In such a mood, it didn't take him long to spot the object of his desire sitting at the bar.

Rich brown complexion, almond-shaped eyes, and full ripe lips caught and held his attention for several moments until he noted her pearls and the long black tux blazer over a white top, both of which failed to conceal her curves. Her black miniskirt gave view to long, shapely legs; her black strappy high heels gave adequate view to a well-done pedicure. Business-casual attire for some intriguing occupation, he thought. And in the right age range. *The perfect specimen . . .*

The stools on either side of the woman were empty. She was drinking something that looked to him like liquid fire. Hendrick tried to shift the majority of his focus to it rather than give the impression that he was leering as he approached and cleared his throat.

"So, uh . . . What's your pleasure?"

She barely turned her head in his direction as her eyes narrowed. "Excuse me?"

"What are you drinking?"

She turned her head more fully in his direction, likely so he could get a better look at her annoyed expression. "Are you serious?"

"Uh . . . I think so."

"It's one of the bar's signature cocktails." She frowned as she looked him up and down. "Do you not come here often?"

His lips parted but said nothing. Had he misjudged? Was this woman a local? Or was he just really out of place, too far out of his element? Maybe all the alcohol he'd consumed this evening had gone to his head in a way he hadn't felt, making him think he could approach a woman way out of his league.

He thought to excuse himself, tossing a "Sorry to bother you" her way, but his voice caught in his throat. He remembered why he had come. Tonight was not the night to take a coward's way out. He cleared his throat and offered a broad smile.

"As a matter of fact, I don't come here often. Never before, in fact." He nodded toward her glass. "Do you recommend it?"

She shrugged. "Depends on how you feel about vegetables."

He tried not to sound unctuous as he said, "I feel they do a body good."

"Well, this certainly does." Her voice had softened. Whatever she'd heard, she chose to take the innocent meaning in his words. "It's beet juice and carrot juice. Ginger. Honey lemonade. Vodka, of course. And a few other things. Maybe a touch of absinthe. I forget the exact ingredients. And the name of it."

"Oh?" He arched his eyebrows in a joking manner. "Do you not come here often?"

She chuckled. "I pass through from time to time." She

waved her hand in a slight, delicate manner toward the empty stool closest to them both—a subtle invitation.

"Well, looks like I just happened to pass through at the right time."

He sat, and they exchanged introductions—Joylynn and Hendrick—before going on to talk for an hour, discussing drinks and local attractions before moving on to their respective professions. She wasn't repulsed by his, and he was fascinated by hers—executive at a candy manufacturer that had been around for over a hundred years. All the while, they ordered more drinks; he tried her healthy recommendations, and she sampled his scotch preferences before reverting back to her own vegetable-based concoctions. The conversation swerved into personal likes and dislikes before one of them blurted, "Let's get out of here."

There was a pause in conversation as they gazed deeply into each other's eyes. Hendrick—buzzed, not drunk—was searching for sincerity and wondering if this was, in fact, the one, the one woman with whom he could make a connection, with whom he could make a legally binding bond, and with whom he could make a child or two. He'd detected no serious flaws, nothing to put him off, and more than a few things that made him consider relocating to wherever she lived, start anew in his profession there.

"Shall we go back to your place?"

Though slurred, her words echoed in his head.

"No," he said. "Let's go to yours."

"Yeah . . . I guess that does make more sense. Since it's here."

As he paid their tab, Hendrick hoped she wasn't drunk. Drunken sex was never good—not enjoyable or a good indicator of how one performed when sober and truly into it. But by the time they got to her room, she seemed as bright and energetic as a woman who'd just finished the last drop of her morning coffee. This, Hendrick thought, could be the beginning of a wonderful new life.

THE SEX WAS wonderful but not all that new. Her dirty talk during the act was certainly different than what he was used to —and welcome, even stimulating. But the motions, their movements together . . . He had to put in much of the work to ensure the two of them flowed with one another. It was worth it, but . . .

Heading home early on Sunday morning, he wondered if he could do better. If what Joylynn had told him about herself was true, she was certainly a catch. But could he catch someone who was a bit more skilled in bed?

As the week went on, he kept in touch, texting Joylynn at least twice a day to keep himself fresh in her mind. She was on his mind constantly, most intensely when he got up early in the mornings to work out. But by Thursday evening, after another upgrade in his wardrobe, he was ready to try his luck again.

He followed a similar circuit, hitting different bars this time —and even a lounge unaffiliated with a hotel—before he found a reasonably young and somewhat sophisticated beauty with whom he could connect.

Ursula was in finance.

Again, Hendrick found the sex to be wonderful.

But something was missing.

He kept in touch with her, of course. She could wind up being the one for him after all. In the meantime, he began another circuit the following Thursday.

He'd stopped his therapy sessions with Klavdiya. He didn't need them anymore. His personal life was finally on the right track. He'd adopted new routines of morning workouts, healthier meals, and smarter shopping. The money he normally would have dedicated to his cuddle bunny now went toward clothes and accessories—dapper threads to dress the new man, the more serious man. The man seriously on the hunt for the one and only woman for him.

But she was elusive.

As the weeks drew on, he went from woman to woman, always thinking he could do better, knowing with certainty he deserved better. Finding the right class of fertile women, talking to them, wooing them—he sharpened his skills with each outing and had less and less trouble getting them under the sheets for a deeper inspection. On the outside, they were all perfect in their own way. Statuesque. Tall and toned. Some had delicate builds; others were athletic yet buxom. Above the shoulders, they ranged from baby faced to heart-shaped beauties. Their faces were expressive, elegant, and ethereal. Top-earning professionals all.

With each one, however, he felt a small sense of absence on the morning after, a sense that only grew in the subsequent days, pushing him to become more and more of an absence in their lives. With a sad-and-mad chuckle at the idea he might never reach his goal, he began referring to the women as *pump-and-dumps*. After each one he pumped (and some of them he graced twice), he had no choice but to dump them. Let them get on with their lives, find someone more appropriate, while he did the same.

He eventually concluded that he was looking in the wrong places. It was time to up his game. He was ready to move beyond out-of-towners and try himself on some of the city's movers and shakers. He did his research and happened upon the sort of spot that was sure to have exactly what he was looking for.

The Edenist was an exclusive, underground club located in the depths of a building that also housed an indoor garden and sculpture museum. Hours after the building's above-ground establishments closed for the day, the club opened its doors. In such a location, the place (according to what he read) never got too raucous; but it allegedly attracted some of the hottest singles in the area.

It cost a pretty penny to gain entrance, but he figured it was worth it. He was determined to make it worth it. If any place catered to the type of women he deserved, this would be it.

Trance music engulfed him as he walked the corridor leading to the main entrance. Not his preferred genre, but certainly closer to his preferences than classical. Close enough to relax him as he entered the club proper and maneuvered through gyrating bodies engulfed in a foggy darkness pierced repeatedly by long, colorful blades of strobing lights.

It took some time, but he managed to get to an elevated position that allowed him some breathing space and a fairly good view of most of the interior. Three well-lit bars captured his attention, primarily for the large murals behind each.

One featured a grand scene of children and cherubs playing games in Heaven. Another, men and women dancing at a grand outdoor festival. The third appeared to his eyes as a massive orgy in what he assumed was one of Hell's valleys—masses of naked men and women entangled with one another amid reddish-brown flames and rocks.

The third mural captivated him, so much so that he never once averted his gaze as he wove through the throngs of people to reach the bar in front of it.

Every stool at the bar was taken, but he had no interest in sitting. He stood not too close behind the row of those seated as he scanned the mural, studying the frozen faces and bodies of those caught up in the throes of underworld ecstasy.

"Interesting, isn't it?"

Through the music and added layers of partygoers' whoops and hollers, a sultry voice reached him. He gradually lowered his chin, setting his eyes on the woman who'd turned around on her stool to address him even as people continually passed between them.

A svelte woman with a pixie cut dyed three different shades, she wore a dress that seemed too conservative for the environment—more nunnery than Edenist. But she'd an enticing smile.

Hendrick closed the distance between them.

"Wanton lovemaking," she said, "on a barren wasteland."

He cocked his head.

With her thumb, she pointed backward toward the mural.

"Oh." He chuckled. "Yeah. I thought it was Hell."

"Interesting. I'd always thought it might be a historical scene. A group of people, a village maybe, whose land has dried up, who've lost their source of food, whose connection to the outside world, to any means of help, has been cut . . . They know they don't have much longer to survive, so why not make love? Recklessly. Go out with a bang." She pressed her lips together and giggled. "I'm Bianca."

He nodded. "Hendrick. Pleasure."

She again pressed her lips together and giggled. "I'll show you pleasure." She slid off her stool to her feet. "Let's dance."

"Uh, I'm not really a dancer." A silly thing to say, he knew even as he said it. Why else would he come to a dance club? "I mean, tonight. I just came here to—"

"I *know* what you're here for. C'mon!"

Bianca grabbed his arm and pulled him through the crowd of drinkers and minglers into the horde of trancers.

She engaged him in a tasteful yet sensual dance. It didn't take him long to find his groove. After an uncounted number of minutes, they stopped to find a table where they could catch their breath enough to drink and talk some more.

Hendrick found the woman pleasant. He thought she seemed to enjoy his company; she certainly seemed to enjoy her cocktails. The more they drank, the more they danced, and the more she seemed to grow attached to him. He glanced at other women, but his attention kept coming back to her. Hers never left him.

"Should we get out of here?" he eventually asked. They had just sat down after their fourth round of dancing.

"Yeah," she said breathlessly. "Let's go upstairs."

His brow furrowed as he reached for his wallet. "Upstairs?"

"Yeah. I told you, I'm a lifetime member of the association . . . We can go for a little private tour."

He'd no idea what she meant but wondered if the building housed apartments on the upper levels. Maybe she lived in one of them.

While one of the bartenders processed his card, Bianca kept talking, mostly about art and her memberships in various organizations around town. Nothing about her intentions for the evening. It was only after he signed the credit card receipt and followed her through a back exit to an elevator that he started to do the math.

He didn't remember her mentioning anything about an "association" while they were talking or dancing, but she had mentioned how fond she was of the sculptures in the building above. She visited them often. His alcohol-clouded mind couldn't remember if he'd said anything about not being familiar with the premises. He wasn't one to haunt museums or gardens or anything artistic. Whether he'd said it or not, she likely picked up on it.

It took a few tries after they stepped onto the elevator, but Bianca eventually managed to steady her hand enough to slide a key card into a slot; she then pressed a button for a higher level.

As the car ascended, she swayed and gyrated, as if she could still hear the music. Here, under better if not-bright-enough lighting, Hendrick took new stock of her. She was certainly attractive, but was this a woman with whom he wanted to spend any significant amount of time?

Once the elevator slid open, she twirled outward as if beginning a new dance, in a new style.

He stuffed his hands in his slacks pockets and followed at a respectable distance, even as she settled into walking—though he considered *swerving* might be a better description of her movements.

She led him through dim, airy spaces—wide and narrow areas of wooden floors and high ceilings loosely populated with headless figures on pedestals, each of them bent, stretched, and variously contorted to pose in stances unnatural for any human being, except those in the most extreme agony or the throes of sublime ecstasy.

If only there were some noises of joy to accompany them now, he thought. The only sounds as they passed through were their joint footsteps and a lone voice—hers.

Caring nothing for art, sculptures least of all, he stayed silent as she commented on and sometimes explained the pieces. He did smile when she turned her face or even spun her whole body in his direction—grinning, gesticulating—looking for and desiring some confirmation or appreciation of some-thing she was saying, something she was explaining, something she was trying to teach him. The moment her eyes left him—drifting or flicking away to land on some new grotesque, head-less piece—his teeth ground. His smile melted into a grimace. The hair crawled on his scalp.

She was intent on lecturing him. Talking down to him.

Mocking him. The more she went on, the more he was convinced her sole purpose in luring him from the Edenist was to belittle him.

Even when they were in the club, he'd thought her talk innocuous. He'd listened, tolerated it, because he thought she was a genuinely smart woman who happened to be inebriated and that was just her way of flirting, talking sexy, cutting loose. He'd hoped she had more to offer him. He was still hoping, but his optimism was losing gas.

Presently, they descended a wide U-shaped staircase; he followed her by two stairs. It struck him that this was how she liked it, wanted it. Him following her as she descended. Him trailing her as she gave herself away, all her knowledge in a place where she was most comfortable, opening herself to him . . .

Once her feet hit the floor, she glided into a space that was equal parts sculptures and plants. She was content to talk to him over her shoulder or just raise her voice as she launched into full docent mode.

He recalled the mural in front of which she'd planted herself in the club. Pieces of its scene rose more vividly in his memory.

Bianca, interpreter of the mural—*wanton lovemaking on a barren wasteland*—guiding him through another land, a land she explained but which he felt—he knew—he must interpret for her. It was what she wanted. It was why she'd brought him.

She wasn't belittling him but beguiling him. Attempting to enchant. Seduce.

As she chirped on, he tried to take greater note of their surroundings. They navigated shrubbery trimmed to resemble human figures, animals, and numerous recognizable shapes. The sculpted objects of marble, wood, and metals became more and more abstract, partially hidden or framed by the abundant greenery and sporadic patches of varicolored blossoms.

Instinctually, he took deeper breaths, inhaling through his nostrils. The flowers . . . Their aromas swam with his senses, taking his mind back to more innocent, guiltlessly pleasurable days . . .

He refocused on Bianca. She was several dozen paces away from him now, her back turned as she expounded on some piece—five crisscrossing Vs entangled in vines and speckled with carnations.

His steps quickened to catch up with her.

When he was just a few feet away, she turned to face him, simpering. "Is any of this making sense to you?"

He grabbed her by the shoulders and forced his lips against hers.

Bianca jerked her head back and screeched. She raised her hands, shoved at his stomach and chest—but he lowered his grip to her elbows, pressed her arms against her sides.

When she kicked at his legs, his old wrestling instincts took over, took advantage of her lack of balance. Lowering his hips, he shifted his weight and forced her to the ground.

Every moment her lips were away from his, she cursed, shrieked, or spat at him.

Every moment he couldn't kiss or nip her lips, he barked.

"*Stop* it. Shut *up*. You know you want this." She wanted him to give her an experience of Eden. "Why the hell else would you have brought me here? This was all under *your* control."

He straddled her, keeping her hips pinned. Memories strobed in his mind, flashing between steamy scenes with girls back when he was in school and the hot snippets from the Edenist's infernal mural. He was going to give Bianca what they both wanted, what they both deserved: raw sex in a faux raw setting, similar to something she'd been chirping about while leading him through this twisted garden.

She stopped shrieking. Her curses were no longer as loud or as frequent. Both changes were signs that she was accepting, acquiescing, easing into what she'd teased him to do. He hoped the frantically violent activity of her hands and arms would soon follow suit—unless that's the way she liked it, wanted it.

He alternated clawing at her dress and swatting her hands away as she clawed at him in turn, reaching for his face. He was okay with the rough stuff, but he wouldn't allow her to draw blood.

He grunted, "Still want control, huh? Well, let's get ourselves a bit more comfortable so we can wrangle properly." Two naked beasts . . .

He shifted his position to lift up her dress, relieving some of his weight from her. With a sudden thrust that seemed to have twice her weight behind it, she heaved him off completely.

He was surprised to find he landed flat on his back, even more surprised to find she'd gotten to her feet faster than he.

He followed as best he could as she weaved between sculptures, slipping in and out of the greenery, until she went behind one large structure of palm fronds and metallic squiggles and didn't reappear.

Panting, he circled the entire piece but saw no sign of her. He stopped, tried to still his breath, and listened—but he didn't hear her. Not her breaths. Not her footsteps.

He released a loud sigh. She knew this place like the back of her hand. She could run and keep up her silly game of hide-and-seek, lure-and-seduce for hours.

"Stupid slut. Not even worth it."

It was late, and he was too tired for games. Whatever allure she'd held was spent. His only desire now was to seek out the exit.

HENDRICK WAS THROUGH WITH DATING—FOR a while, at least.

For the next couple of weeks, he put his head down and focused on his profession, the operations of his business—so much so that he slackened on his morning exercises and was less picky about the sorts of foods he put into his body. His craving for sweets returned with a vengeance.

In spare moments of reflection—often as he lay in bed at night, alone—he wondered if he should just give up. Maybe the life he wanted—the one he deserved—wasn't for him. But each morning, usually before he even turned off his alarm, he resolved to keep going. He had one life to live, and he was determined to live it on his terms.

His biological clock was ticking, though. He needed to figure out what he was doing wrong and fix it. *Fast.*

Entering his third week of all work and no play, he considered returning to the Warren. Maybe he'd see Klavdiya again. Or maybe he'd try one of the therapies the other bunnies offered. Wednesday night, as he considered his weekend plans, he received an invitation via text.

Saturday Night. 42nd and Wheaton. Red Door. Blue Light. 10ish.

He didn't recognize the sender's number, but a follow-up text claimed the sender was a woman he'd recently met, one with whom he'd enjoyed a spectacular coupling. The invitation was to an event where even more pleasurable activities would take place, where participants would experience ecstasies that would make them feel young again, revitalized.

He tried calling the number to verify the woman's identity, but it rang incessantly, offering no opportunity to leave a voice mail. Text was his only means of communication.

So he texted back: *Who R U?*

U will C was the response.

Can u give a hint?

He received emojis of a carrot and a beet.

It took only seconds for him to recall the candy company executive—*Joylynn*. He well remembered his experience with her. A fun evening, an even more pleasurable night. Why not see if there was any magic left between them? It was, after all, entirely plausible a woman intimately involved in making and marketing a product for kids might know a secret or two about rejuvenation.

Thursday morning, he got up an hour early to jump-start his exercise routine. Working through his fifth set of a hundred pushups, he pondered whether he should just try to squeeze into one of the outfits he'd purchased after meeting Joylynn the first time. Working through his sixth and final set of pushups, he concluded the shape of his body had changed too much, and he didn't trust whatever exercise-and-diet routine he could manage in the next two days to make a big difference. He'd shop for a new outfit on Saturday morning.

Saturday night, a little after nine thirty, he arrived where instructed.

In a silk suit minus a tie, he walked up and down the sidewalks that led to and from where 42nd Street met Wheaton Avenue, nonchalantly at first, getting a feel for the area, an idea of the sorts of people who populated the sidewalks at this hour as well as the types of establishments that lined the streets, both of which could give hints as to the type of spot in which he'd be meeting Joylynn. All the while, he kept an eye out for the red door, the blue light.

He saw no signs of either.

He rechecked the text messages he'd exchanged with Joylynn. Had he forgotten something? Overlooked something?

No. 42nd and Wheaton. Red Door. Blue Light.

It was now five past ten. He retraced his steps, hurrying up and down the same sidewalks, occasionally stopping passersby to ask if they knew of or had seen any red doors. Those who didn't ignore or push away from him just shook their heads.

At fifteen past ten, he pulled his phone out of his suit jacket's pocket.

He was about to dash off a text to Joylynn when the back of his neck tingled. He looked up from his phone and to his right, toward the walkable gap between two buildings. *An alley.*

Of course the door leading to such a rendezvous would not be visible from the street.

Of course he wouldn't get lucky with the first alley he checked. The narrow but decently lit passageway had two doors—neither of them red.

The second alley, the one across the street, held the prize. Maneuvering around crumpled paper bags, broken bottles, flattened and stained cardboard boxes, puddles, and a few mice, he found a red door. But no blue light.

There was a wall-mounted bulb above the door but, turned off, it was impossible for him to determine its hue. He tried the door's handle and found it locked.

Looking left and right down the alley, toward the distant bordering sidewalks, he wondered if any other invitees might be coming, one of whom might have a greater clue as to how to gain entry. But after more than four minutes passed, he remained alone.

He thought to text Joylynn for further instructions when he heard a buzz coming from the door's handle. A moment later, the light above the door switched on. A dim blue light. When he tried the handle again, it turned.

After walking a few steps into an empty, carpeted hallway lit from above by fluorescent lights, he hesitated. There were no greeters. No bouncers. No one to guide him. Behind him, the door swung shut and clicked as it locked again. Was he late? Were all the other invitees already at the gathering, well into the festivities? Was the party already in full swing?

Whether it was or not—*where* was it? He heard no revelers and saw no trace of anyone having passed down the hallway before him.

There were a few doors lining the corridor. He tried the knob of each he passed, only to find them locked. He again thought to text Joylynn, but he had no signal.

With a sigh, he continued forward, eventually quickening his pace through the gently declining passageway once he realized that, wherever he was going, his destination was at the far end. He went on for eight or nine minutes until he reached it, finding himself in front of an elevator. Seeing no other option for progress, he thumbed the button next to the door, which slid open immediately.

Inside the car, there was only one button. He shrugged and pressed it. The car moved downward for almost five minutes before the door again slid open, revealing another passageway.

Recessed lights cast an amber glow on the bare concrete walls and floor. His footsteps echoed as he proceeded, his eyes alert for doors, gates, or other possible openings on either side of the straight corridor. He found none. But aromas of vanilla and chocolate found his nostrils.

This is going to be some party, he thought.

Incorporating strawberry and other fruits, the sweet scents grew stronger as he went along. Wherever he was going to wind up, food was involved. Something decadent. Maybe Joylynn and her friends were food fetishists. The treated, sweetened human body as a type of aphrodisiac—chocolates and bananas —to be enjoyed before being consumed . . .

He kept on, at times closing his eyes—reveling in the

aromas, fantasizing, his tongue moistening—dimly aware the corridor was steadily darkening.

His steps felt lighter. His eyelids, heavier. In near darkness, he almost seemed to skate forward—gliding in the gloom—until he stumbled on uneven flooring.

Steadying himself, his eyes widened as he slowly turned in a circle. He was no longer in a corridor. The aromas had lulled him into a place where no walls or ceiling were visible. He stood in a broad area illumed with yellowish light from a source he couldn't determine but could only assume came from above. He tried without success to see anything beyond the semidistant shadows at the fringe of his surroundings.

"Hello?" His tentative greeting echoed. "Is this where the action is?"

He heard nothing but his own voice. All around, however, the shadows stirred.

"Hello?" His second attempt was more uncertain. "Is anyone there?"

The shadows became more agitated. Though as impenetrable to sight as before, it was clear they were drawing nearer, tightening Hendrick's circle of light.

The air plunged in temperature as he again turned, looking every which way for a possible escape.

"This isn't funny." His voice was tremulous.

When the encroaching blackness seemed only a few dozen paces away on every side of him, his teeth began to chatter. The inner and outer forces of anxiousness and freezing air shivered him. His leg muscles twitched. His body wanted to run. His mind soon agreed. Rather than allowing himself to be shaken into stillness, he resolved to take control of his body. He was no coward, not one to let himself be overtaken.

He hunched his shoulders and bent his legs, preparing to

thrust himself forward, readying himself to tackle anything he might encounter while running blind.

Sudden gusts of warm air made him hesitate.

The shadows dissipated—vanishing as quickly as the temperature rose—revealing an immense vaulted chamber, of which he was not the sole occupant. In their wake, the shadows had left several standing figures.

Women.

A dozen of them—maybe thirty feet away—were fanned out before him. Slowly and silently, on feet sheathed in tight-fitting slippers, they converged on him.

Their faces were hidden behind masks. Hendrick only knew they were women from their curves. Their hips. Their breasts. Their nakedness barely hidden by gowns sheer enough to appear spectral, as if the women were cloaked in barely visible auras.

Heartened, his posture straightened. He was certainly in the right place. This was going to be a wild time. But his muscles again twitched. He wondered what sort of kink these women might be into. Their silvery masks were bestial. *Rodents . . .*

His stomach fluttered as his mind raced with possibilities. They were underground, after all. The sweet aromas he'd smelled earlier were now a memory but a prominent one as he considered what attracted rodents and what rodents did once they reached the source of attraction. *Gnawing. Rending. Chewing.*

Joylynn . . . He tried to remember if she'd ever mentioned any weird fetishes, any dark fantasies, any twisted perversions, but his attempts at straight lines of thought rapidly became tangled.

He attempted to laugh away his nervousness, his silliness. His body wanted to turn and run, but he fought it. What kind of man would run from women—*only* women—who had bodies like these approaching him?

His anxious body fought back against his mind, resulting in him stumbling a few feet forward, backward, and to the side as the women drew closer. But he didn't run.

Soon the only part of him that moved quickly were his eyes, examining each woman as they tightened into a semicircle in front of him. Twelve women, bathed in silken luminescence, adorned with chrome-plated masks—rabbit masks, clean and clear enough to send back a distorted reflection whenever he set his eyes on one. The masks' ears were folded backward and down, covering the back of the head, making the masks more like helmets in design.

He tried to swallow, but his throat caught. Helmets implied rough-and-tumble sport. Dangerous play.

The women stopped advancing when they were less than a dozen feet from him. Hidden faces notwithstanding, they were all beautiful in their own way. Voluptuous. Statuesque. Lithe. Toned.

None said a word. He guessed they were waiting for him to speak first.

After two attempts, he successfully cleared his throat. "So, uh, do I get my pick?"

"You have already had it." A familiar voice resounded, filling the chamber. "Over and over." It wasn't Joylynn.

Hendrick looked up and to the right, toward the source of the noise. Amid shadows, a muted blue light steadily brightened, giving view to a thick ledge of brick. Just beyond it, he glimpsed the upper half of a dark entryway. The speaker was likely shrouded within.

But only for a moment.

The blue light took on purplish hues as the woman emerged to stand at the precipice of the ledge. She wore a nurse's scrub dress, its white fabric remaining white, resisting any blemish, even as the woman's head and exposed arms were engulfed in a periwinkle radiance.

"Klavdiya . . . ?"

She gazed down at him with a frown. Equally beautiful and strange—the light made her appear as one who'd emerged from the depths of the ocean or from some other poorly explored realm.

"What are you doing here?"

"I'm here to oversee your initiation. As the text said, you've been invited to join a club. A very exclusive club."

In unison, the women lifted their helmets. He recognized the faces instantly. Joylynn was among them. As was Ursula. Bianca . . .

All of them—each of them—were women he'd been with since his last appointment with Klavdiya.

He swallowed several times before he could manage, "The hell is all this?"

"Therapy."

He snorted. "I've already had my final session with you."

"You did. Then you went on to have several more with other—to use a term—*cuddle bunnies*."

His eyes raced back and forth across the stony faces of the women before him. They silently glared back.

"No way you all work at the Warren." He muttered the words, then shook his head, repeating them silently, before shouting, "No *way*."

The women's lips remained tight. Hendrick's words weren't really for them anyway. He was only trying to convince himself while also hurling an accusation at Klavdiya. She had to be lying.

"I wondered," Klavdiya said, "how many of them you

would go through before you came to true terms with yourself. Your true self. But you never saw your true self."

True, repeated. Tripled. Hendrick took it as a response to his accusation. But he still couldn't believe it.

"Before our last session," Klavdiya said, "it was true that women—the women you thought you deserved—were rejecting you because you weren't up to their standards. But it had little to do with your profession or how you looked. It was your odious ways. Outward trappings had nothing to do with you being a slob. That's simply what you are, deep down."

From deep down, anger slowly welled up, making him feel as if his entire body were pulsing, expanding and contracting at an increasing rate.

"You were never fat. Overweight. Obese. You just saw yourself as others saw you: someone who wanted something beyond what he deserved. I believed you didn't deserve the women you wanted because you lacked confidence. So, at our previous session, I *gave* you confidence—and you squandered it. You violated another . . . attempted to. Now you deserve something else."

"No . . . *No*. It isn't fair. You sent these women out to meet me. They were *plants*. They were sent out to pick me. Hell, deep down I probably even knew that. I always knew something wasn't quite right with them." He looked at them, meeting each one's gaze as he pleaded. "It's not my fault it didn't work out with any of you. I was set up. It wasn't supposed to work out."

"You were set up," Klavdiya said. "I set you up. But the outcome is your fault and yours alone. You could have chosen any of them. Made your life 'complete,' as you saw it. While giving them a new life as well."

Bitterly, he chortled. "What? A new life for a whore? Is that what you all are into? Trying to find a man with some money that you can get your claws into? One who'll take care of you? Screw you—*all* of you."

"You did," Klavdiya said. "And now it's time to discuss your final payment."

In unison, the women stepped forward.

With only a breath's hesitation, Hendrick turned and ran, stumbling just once as he spotted the entrance to the corridor that had led him here and dashed for it.

Several steps into the corridor, he realized it was different. It wasn't a straight path. It wound to the left, then turned abruptly to the right. But he didn't stop moving. Though no one chased him (as far as he could tell), he ran as fast as he could manage down curves and around corners that had not existed previously.

He considered that maybe there were several similar passageways that led to the chamber. He'd entered through one straight and narrow but had turned to flee down a different one. He wondered whether he should backtrack, risk confronting the women again for the potential reward of finding the straightest possible route away from them.

He slowed as he considered, only to have a fetid smell hit his nostrils. Raw sewage. He looked around for any signs of waste matter, dark liquids. But the walls—the flooring—showed no sign. All were uniform. Spotless gray.

Up ahead, the corridor veered to the right. He quickened his steps, hoping to outrun the stench. But shortly after rounding the corner, he stopped short.

Before him sat a glistening brownish-gray mass about five feet wide. Hendrick didn't move as its front portion slowly stretched upward, rising more than six feet, a height steadily made taller by two antennae that protruded from the top.

Fear seemed to paralyze Hendrick below the neck, but his mouth widened as far as it would go to unleash a scream.

Just below the slimy creature's antennae, slick-sticky folds of its skin peeled back, revealing a gaping hole lined all the way around with what appeared to be rusty spikes. From somewhere within the depths of the hole came a dull roar. The creature was imitating him or mocking him. Or attempting to communicate.

Hendrick's jaw remained slack. He no longer screamed, just loitered in fear.

But when several appendages lifted flat up off the creature's body and jolted toward him, survival instinct spun Hendrick around and sent him dashing back in the direction from which he'd come.

He was done with screaming. He needed as much oxygen as he could get to keep his legs moving.

They slowed, however, as he turned a corner and slowed further when, up ahead, the corridor forked into three. The tunnel branched where it hadn't before.

It didn't matter. All that mattered was that he put distance between himself and the creature. Eventually he would find a way out.

He stopped only to remove and toss his suit's jacket.

On a whim, he chose a path and hustled, running for a solid minute, not even slowing when the stench of sewage flooded his nostrils.

Turning a corner, however, he was forced to stop. Another greasy slug, bigger than a man, confronted him.

As the creature lurched forward, he ran the other way, fighting for good, clean breaths while he retraced his steps. Or attempted to.

No matter which way he ran, nothing about the corridors seemed familiar other than the leaden walls. Not once did he run down the same path where he'd discarded his jacket.

He did, however, confront another giant slug, which sent him panting down another path, only to confront another.

At one point, he unbuttoned and tossed his dress shirt, heavy with sweat, hoping its loss would lighten his burden. The effect was brief. He took off his shoes, faintly hoping their loss would make him nimbler. Instead, he felt each pounding step more painfully in his knees.

Huffing, lost, slowed to trotting, he was thankful the slugs had the speed of their miniature counterparts. He didn't think about where they'd come from. Didn't care about what they actually were beyond their appearance. His thoughts, once consumed with escape, now focused as best they could in a muddled mind on searching for—hoping for—a hiding place, a sufficient space where he might recover his strength, stay alive.

But his body was enveloped in humidity, foul odors. The atmosphere of the corridors seemed increasingly that of a tropical realm of rotten fruit and exotic animal carcasses. His eyesight lost strength in proportion to his legs. With a heaving chest, he stumbled forward into darkness until he tripped on his own feet and fell to the concrete.

Drenched with sweat, his knees and elbows scraped and likely bleeding, he remained where he was, attempting to get his lungs under control as the area around him gradually brightened. Sensing movement in front of him, he lifted his tired head.

Joylynn, Bianca, and the ten other women were arrayed before him. He was in the same chamber, as if he'd never turned away from them. As if he'd never run.

The women held their helmets at waist level, giving him eye-level reflections of himself—a grotesque mess.

Directly in front of him, the women parted, allowing space to Klavdiya, who'd left her lofty position to now stand before him and sneer.

Mustering what strength he could, Hendrick tried pushing himself up to a standing position, but his extremities tingled as if millions of minuscule crystals were perpetually exploding under the skin.

His body collapsed into a seated position.

He tried again, tried to battle against the numbness—but he only found comfort on his knees, kneeling before Klavdiya. Kneeling before all the women.

"I invited you to join a club," Klavdiya said. "I, in fact, began the initiation months ago. It—*you*—could have turned out very differently. But your actions dictate what you're destined to become."

A burning sensation flared on the back of his hands. He raised them before his eyes.

A field of whiteheads had sprouted amid a brownish-red patch on the back of his hands—a rash that rapidly spread to his fingers, up his arm. To the touch, his skin felt raw, pimply. His palms were pale, displaying a lack of color that was soon replaced by a grayish hue.

He glanced at the mirroring helmets the women still held at waist level. His head not only appeared misshapen; it felt that way. His face had taken on a brownish-gray tone—as had his now-glistening hands. To the touch, his face was viscid. He examined his fingertips, hoping for the rainbow sheen he'd seen before his last session with Klavdiya, wishing for a sign that he could go back to that time, start over. But there was no rainbow, only whorls of gray, brown, green, and black. There was no returning.

"You *have* returned."

Klavdiya seemed to read his mind. Hendrick raised his chin to meet her gaze.

"These . . ." She gestured toward the far reaches, the walls and the ceiling. "These are the bowels of the Warren. The nice part of them anyway.

"And these nice women? The female and male cuddle bunnies who conduct their therapies and work their magic in the holes aboveground? Well, we all have reasons for doing what we do. The Warren has always been about the promise of renewal. Vitality. Resurrection."

His gaze left Klavdiya's face to view the other women's as they contorted, seemed to melt. In little time, their visages appeared as distorted as his had in their reflective masks—but they went further, continuing to change as their bodies did the same.

"It's the cycle," Klavdiya continued. "We give to receive. And when the ideal happens, when the promise is fulfilled, therapist and client are joined together in a new life, one that is mutually fulfilling."

The women on either side of her had aged, greatly—almost beyond recognition. If Hendrick had to guess, he would have placed each of them well over a hundred years old, well beyond the age of all but the rarest humans. He'd no idea how they were still standing, breathing. To him, they were animate corpses, straddling life and death.

His innards churned as he recalled the history of the Warren, the full history. *A circle of wealthy old friends formed a pact and initiated the project . . .*

"These women, for too long they've had no loved ones in their lives. You loved them, in your way. But you were no better than those who came before you or those who came before them."

The Haracomb's residents—*resurrected and transformed . . .*

As his throat constricted, Hendrick breathed the word. "*Witches.*"

Klavdiya shook her head. "Now, now—you're in no position

to name call." She and the other women stepped backward. "You're in a position—the proper position for you—because you know, deep down, that the dumps is where you're supposed to be. Your actions have shown that, in abundance."

The women continued to back away as the internal systems of his organs and bones, his blood vessels and nerves, were all caught up in an intrusive new system of violent winds, an interior cyclone that tested the stability of what his body had known for over forty years as its only truth.

"There are deeper realms of our abode. Places where all the waste from the bathrooms and other rooms end up. We have a staff who have dedicated what remains of their lives, their bodies, to recycling those materials into products we can use. They—and now you—shall live only to consume."

Shadows moved forward to envelop the receding women as Hendrick felt increasingly bloated. What clothes remained on him tightened, then ripped.

From behind him came a chorus of dull roars as several sluglike creatures drew nearer. Welling up from deep inside him, a prolonged roar responded while his body pulsed—expanding in beats, never contracting.

"There you go," Klavdiya said as the women disappeared from his view. "*Relax* and *release*."

What should have been painful was pleasurable. He didn't move his position, just experienced a frisson of delight—over and over—while in place.

As his body remade itself, he felt increasingly revitalized. And hungry.

Intense aromas of flowers and herbs swam with his new senses, agitating cravings he was anxious to fulfill.

EUPHORIA, OR LOVE ON THE ROCKS

"What you'll feel as pleasure will be a false sensation. A dangerous illusion."

In her youth, Kelsi had often wondered about her caretaker's oft-repeated words. But once she broke free from the old woman's influence and began to discover the true joys of life for herself, she easily concluded that the one who raised her had just never experienced the ecstasy of a perfect coupling.

Kelsi had just experienced one of her best yet. Her body had been like a bushy plant—one showered in warm lights, dazzled with colors, while rapidly erupting with thousands of flowers—budding and blooming in a matter of seconds, over and over—each of them visited by a fluttering mass—minuscule sippers of nectar—their flickering tongues inciting further excitations. The tremors gradually settled in the area of her throat, inducing a cry that bled into a song.

Her voice blended with those of her surrounding brothers and sisters, all of them swaying, standing nearly an inch deep in a field once dry but now oversaturated—the result of their orgiastic endeavor.

After the usual rounds of hugging and embracing, they'd sloshed out of the reddish-brown field together—arms joined, singing, their voices lifted to join with the perfumed winds, which carried their song over a good portion of the living land. A song of praise. A song of thanksgiving. A song expressing how thankful they were to be alive, and how happy they were to do their part to sustain their Giver-Receiver.

Kelsi grinned as she walked the gravel path now, recalling how she'd been taught that each successive coupling would seem more pleasurable than the last. She'd experience increasing levels of joy—until she didn't. She'd plateau. Her body would become tolerant. Shortly thereafter, the couplings would become less pleasurable. Eventually, they'd be pure torture. Her body would become decrepit, betraying the marks of one who was in disagreement with her younger nature and no longer fully in tune with her environment. She'd be forced to move on, assume the role of a caretaker—a fate she considered worse than oblivion.

She regarded a few of them now, five elders standing tall among the knee-high plants and the dozens of young ones scurrying about. In the lush fields on either side of the path that she and her siblings walked, the caretakers paced slowly, instructing the excited young ones, attempting in loud yet monotone voices to get them to slow down and concentrate so that when they stooped to examine and pluck the peach-hued berries, they'd inflict no damage on the plants, cause no pain to their Giver-Receiver. The experience was one of learning for the immature, not only how to harvest one of the chief ingredients for their meals, but also—in part—how to behave when they reached the age when they would engage in coupling.

Yet the elders wore the same bored expressions they never tired of displaying. The elders were beyond mature, almost beyond life itself. They no longer sang. They no longer danced.

They were unable to experience joy. But they were content, existing without complaint to harvest the newborns and cultivate the young, adapting them to the ways of the land, teaching them what natural-born instinct couldn't.

Though Kelsi had been taught such a fate was inevitable, she'd long ago vowed to do everything possible to avoid the caretaker status. And today she believed she'd finally found the key.

"*Hey*—aren't you coming to watch the descent?"

A few of her sisters and brothers had noticed she'd veered away from them.

She waved them away. "I'll catch up." It's not like she'd miss anything. The event was as regular as it was spectacular. And she wasn't really all that particular about which one of the drops she'd claim as her own.

She and her siblings had the rituals they performed together, a series of them. Walking alone down the barely trodden path that wound toward the Resting Forest, she thought she'd start a new ritual of her own.

A collection of partially wooden vessels that had been merged with the bodies of those who were, at present, of no use to the land, the Resting was quite different from the land's other forests. Lacking wildlife yet rampant with twisting indigo shadows, it welcomed only the most reluctant visitors. But after her earlier experience, Kelsi would make a point to come more often, each time with a beatific smile on her face.

After all, the forest was a blessing. Here, the Giver-Receiver had grown vessels with the purpose of harboring those who would wrong it, keeping them safe—preventing them from further harming themselves or the land—until they were ready to be reborn, fit to be utilized, ready and able to serve again.

For the time being, the old bodies were at one with the

vessels, while the essences those bodies once contained flowed about as the dark-fluid shadows of the woods.

Kelsi made her way through the dense collection of grayish-green trees, their branches high and heavy with burgundy leaves, not stumbling once, stopping only when in front of the scaly-barked trunk marking her former caretaker's resting place.

She waited, still and silent, as shadows coiled around the tree, shaking the branches, rustling the leaves, until the combination of shadow and bark produced the vague image of a woman embedded in the trunk. It was all the suspended elder could manage for the time being.

"*Child*," a voice rasped. "What is it?"

Kelsi grinned before recounting, in lavish detail, everything about her earlier coupling. *This* would be her new ritual. After each ecstatic coupling, she'd come here to brag, to enlighten the benighted, maybe even inspire her former caretaker to repent for her past wrongs, help her help herself to be reborn.

Kelsi punctuated her tale with a giggle and sealed it with a tight-and-wide smile.

The tree groaned. "And?"

"*And* I've developed my own technique to ensure it only gets better and better from now on."

Another groan preceded the hiss of "*Foolish* . . ."

"Foolish? I'm not the one relegated to the Resting. I've spent a lot of time thinking about you, about how to avoid becoming like you. And I figured it out. You, like the other elders, never truly understood what you were doing. The repeated ecstasies eventually overwhelmed your bodies because you didn't understand your bodies. You fell out of balance and aged, withered. A particularly sick minority of them were so deep in misunderstanding, they got bad ideas, poisonous ideas. And, well, here you are."

A series of three short groans sounded almost like a laugh. "Reflection is not one of your strengths. It never has been. You are heading precisely down the route that—when you were younger and had more potential—I warned you against taking."

"Good thing I don't remember that bad advice. I'm a free being. And you . . . Well . . . Your time for teaching is over."

"And your time, child, is coming. It will hit you without warning. Then you'll remember everything. And despair."

"I'll remember to keep visiting you, false teacher. Flawed creature. Maybe my repeated visits—me relating my experiences of greater and greater ecstasies—will in some way be instructive to showing you the way, lighting the route to your salvation. For now, I leave you . . . to expect me again."

She departed the forest humming a tune. Stepping onto a more well-worn path, she began toward the overlook, where she'd join her siblings. Together, as a joyous family, they'd witness the descent, pick their chosen, cheerfully argue, and make trades before getting on with their day of tending to the loving land that gave as much as it received.

THE BREEZE TICKLING across Hadrian's bare stomach and chest brought an uneasy smile to his lips even as his eyes remained shut. It was only the sound of crashing waves and the briny scent of sea spray that made his eyelids flutter. A second breeze made him realize what an uncomfortable position his body was actually in.

He lay on something uneven, unyielding . . . Firm, gritty, and moist. His limbs, spread-eagled. His head, turned to lie flat on its left cheek. Fully open, his eyes greeted a collection of large rocks—a mass of boulders. He wasn't alone. He saw three other men, a good distance from him and from one another.

Each was apparently naked, lying on a rock or attempting to sit up. Beyond them, an unbroken expanse of teal water continued on to the horizon.

The sea.

Hadrian stayed put, trying to figure how he'd gotten here, dimly aware of his own beyond-partial nudity. Aching joints and the potential slipperiness of the boulders forced him to move slowly as he twisted his body and repositioned his head to get a look at his nether regions.

Thankfully, he wore bathing trunks.

Easing himself into a sitting position, realization pushed further, brushing away a dusty certainty. He wasn't in his swim trunks. He was in his underwear.

What the hell did I get into last night? What the hell did we get into?

Judging by their movements, the other men seemed to have the same thoughts.

Looking beyond them, and behind himself, he saw the white sands of the beach and other massive clumps of boulders, each of them hosting a collection of men and women. Some remained sprawled; others roused.

After an as-yet-undetermined amount of time spent snoozing on a large, wet rock, he deemed himself lucky he hadn't tumbled off in his sleep, falling down to the sand to break a limb or, twisting another way, getting himself wedged in a gap.

But somehow he'd gotten up on the big rock while wearing next to nothing. He had to have some cuts, scrapes, or bruises from having climbed onto such an inhospitable mass. Checking himself over, however, he found none. His skin was unblemished. Even the marks that had been with him for some time—the scratch marks from fake fingernails, the scar from a well-aimed stiletto heel—were hardly distinguishable. His skin tone was slightly lighter, though. As if he'd been avoiding sunlight for a couple of weeks.

Hard to avoid now, he thought as he tilted his head back, searching the sky for the sun.

He found no hint of the blinding orb. Or even a patch of sky—not overhead anyway.

The sky was abundant with what initially appeared to him as smoke exhaled from a series of immensely tall and equally invisible chimneys. In small, random patches—and only briefly—the dark-gray billowing clouds brightened with neon-like colors of orange, blue, red, and green. Whatever was happening above, it seemed to have little to no effect on the amount of light on the ground. His surroundings were as bright as one would expect on an early summer morning with a cloudless sky.

He turned his attention to the sea. The clouds above did not cover the entire sky—only the land and a good portion of the sea beyond it. He began to wonder whether the clouds' strange colors came from the hidden sun, but his contemplations shifted to the best way of getting himself down.

As he pondered, he took note of the people already down below, on the sand. There were four or five dozen on their feet, alone or in pairs. Several others sprawled in the sand, as if passed out. An almost equal number were on their knees, crawling and scrabbling, as if searching for a lost article: perhaps their keys, perhaps some piece of clothing that had gotten away from them. All were as scantily clad or nude as the people on the rocks. None had any beachgoing accessories. No towels. No umbrellas. Though some appeared to be in trunks or bikinis—and others wore even less—Hadrian guessed few were here to enjoy the sand and waters. Those who were ambulatory and on their own seemed to have more stagger in their step than easygoingness. It wasn't much different with those who walked in pairs; one seemed to be helping their partner maintain a relatively straight course.

The helpers held his attention. They invariably wore towels or skirts around their waists. The men were bare chested; the women—most, but not all—wore bikini tops. All—women and men—had exotically colored hair. Blue and pink. Purple and blue. Purple and pink. Turquoise. Aquamarine. Black, purple, and silver.

Whatever party had happened, whatever celebratory gathering had brought them all here, must've been outrageous. A spicy clambake whose story they all would be telling their friends for years afterward. If only he could remember it.

He likely wasn't the only one. The groans and moans of those on the rocks near him—recovering, trying to get their bearings—were intermittently muffled by the breeze.

He began to call out to the person nearest him, a man in his thirties, to ask for a clue when he caught sight of a stunning woman on the beach walking directly toward him, waving as if he were an old friend.

Barefoot with long legs and fulsome curves, she'd brown skin, a heart-shaped face, and long braids parading several shades of lavender. She wore a bikini top and a ruffle-trimmed wrap skirt.

The woman was merciless in her beauty—but damned if he didn't recognize her.

She stood just below his rock, beaming up at him. "Morn."

"Morning." He responded before considering how odd her greeting was. Her accent, even stranger. He couldn't place it.

Just where in the world did people say "Morn" over "Morning" or "Good morning?"

"Feeling a little stiff, aren't you?"

"Yeah," he said. "Just a little."

"It'll go away."

"You seem to be pretty sure of yourself."

"I'm sure of you," she said with a chuckle. "I'm used to handling drops."

He snorted at the designation. "And just who are you?"

"I'm one of the groundskeepers."

"Groundskeeper?" A grubby maintenance worker—looking like that?

Her head tilted slightly to the left as she fluttered her eyelashes. His facial expression must have made his thoughts plain.

Clearing his throat, he said, "I'm sorry, I just . . ." Losing his words, he cleared his throat again.

"Do you think you can jump down?" she asked. "Without hurting yourself?"

"I wouldn't want to risk it."

"All right, then, c'mon." She gestured as she rounded the boulder. "I'll guide you down. Gently."

His stiff muscles elicited a few grunts, but he managed to stand and obey as she told him exactly where to place his feet and how to move.

Despite not having his perspective, she obviously knew the big rocks well—every gap, every jagged edge, every solid foothold and handhold. She certainly must've had extensive experience with party drops like him as she got him down to the sand as easily as if he'd descended a staircase.

Still, he sighed and stretched once on solid ground and took no steps—not until he realized his assistant was no longer nearby.

The woman now stood a few dozen feet away from the big rocks. She gestured for him to follow her as she turned a shoulder and began walking.

He forced his tight legs to catch up. Glancing about, he noticed other colored-haired women and men talking to the people on rocks, attempting to guide them down safely. It struck him that the helpers he'd seen on the beach were also caretakers of some sort. *Groundskeepers.* Employees of whatever resort he and his fellow partygoers had checked themselves into.

The sand was soft under his bare feet, softer than any sand he'd felt before. A comforting sensation—but he became unsettled once he caught up with the woman.

"Wait. My keys . . ."

"Keys?"

"To my . . . room, I guess. I must've had keys or something with me. I can't imagine I came all the way out here to party without anything on me."

She tee-heed his concern. "You're not leaving anything behind, believe me."

"But—"

"Everything you need will be provided."

She led him up a moderately steep incline where the sand mostly gave way to grass, excepting the pathways that tendrilled through the greenery.

He followed the woman onto one such sandy pathway, which widened as the sand transitioned to densely packed pebbles. Hadrian hesitated before placing his bare feet on these —though after seeing the barefoot woman walk on them without any hint of discomfort, he followed and found the path slightly spongy, almost as if he were stepping on marshmallows rather than rocks.

Checking to ensure he was really walking on stones, he noticed tiny black dots speckling his legs. He tried wiping them off, with no luck.

"Don't worry about those," the woman said. "We'll get them washed off soon."

"Um, okay." He wondered at the implication but put it out

of his mind as they continued on, side by side, down the path. Ahead of them and on adjacent paths were others similarly coupled. The shameful if not painful marches from the scene of debauchery . . . He had the impression such libertine soirees, and the orderly cleanup afterward, were normal here. But how often did they happen? How wild did they often get?

"So how'd you get a job like this?"

"Job?"

"Yeah. What you do here. You said you're a groundskeeper . . ."

"Ah. Yes. Well, I just do what I must."

Hadrian's jaw clenched. Those words—he couldn't easily put their implication out of his mind. Was she what her phrase implied? One step below a willing servant, one step up from a slave? Did this resort, whatever resort into which he'd booked himself, exploit labor? Had she and the others been trafficked in from some unfortunate country and put to work? Or lured with false promises of riches, then brainwashed or threatened into working for pennies?

His mind went wild with theories until he shook his head to push them aside and hold them at bay. He hadn't much to go on, certainly not enough to jump to such conclusions.

"Where exactly are you from?" he asked.

"I'm a native. Born here. From blood and soil, you know."

He didn't know, but her words lent weight to some of his theories.

Before he set out to become her emancipator, though, he thought it wise to get a better idea of just where he was. Their surroundings—while beautiful—were not jogging his memory.

The grasses on either side of their path were less green than they had been closer to the sand; they approached the color of straw.

The occasional breezes caressing his skin seemed musical;

he heard a melody each time they blew past; in their wake they left brief and sweet aromas, redolent of tropical fruit, of which he saw no signs.

The trees he did see were at a fair distance from their path, but they didn't seem the type that bore fruit. Bone white, their high branches were draped with copious amounts of dully sparkling tinsel. To him, they appeared as the skeletal hands and arms of giants—planted and swaying—draped in a collapsed nervous system, still working, still fighting to reanimate the fraction of a body long past help or healing.

Blinking and shaking his head at such a gruesome thought, Hadrian narrowed his eyes at the nearest trees. They soon put him more in the mind of the live oaks from his native Savannah, trees famous for their curtains of Spanish moss. These weren't the same, but similar enough.

But he still wasn't feeling the environment. How long had he been here? Where were his recent memories of the place?

"Where exactly . . . I mean, *what* is this place?"

"What, you mean this part of the island?" the woman said. "We simply refer to it as Reception."

Island . . . So he *was* at a resort. *Good.*

Fantastic, actually. He had finally stopped thinking about it, stopped finding excuses, and had finally pushed the go button on taking a decent vacation. One that he'd been telling himself he deserved, set in some out-of-the-way location. He wondered which of the destinations he'd had in mind that he'd finally settled on.

But his self-satisfaction eroded as he considered his condition.

He'd had hangovers before, but this was taking the cake. His post-drunken brain fog usually just left him feeling unbalanced, with several hours of the most recent events inaccessible. But at present he had no sense of dizziness. The stiffness in muscles and joints—as the woman had promised—was now gone. And so were the last who-knows-how-many days.

Well, the woman was used to drops. No shame in admitting he'd dropped a few memories.

"This island . . . Where is it? I mean, if I'm being honest"—he chuckled—"I don't recall to where I've whisked myself away."

She flashed a condescending smile. "The island has many beautiful names. And such a beautiful history."

"Yeah?"

"The island, it remained lonely for centuries. Until two true lovers met and populated it."

"Let me guess. A man and a woman, both separately ship-wrecked. Or two parachuters who were blown way off course. Or one from both categories."

"It was two giants."

Reflexively, he glanced at the nearest tree. "A giant man and a giant woman?"

"A sea dragon. And the island itself. Amorous and ready to breed."

"*That's* the history?" He stifled the guffaw that surged from his belly. There was no trace of playfulness in the woman's expression. She was serious. Serious in mistaking ridiculous myth for actual events. He couldn't blame her though. Natives all over the world, especially those who hadn't benefitted from modern Western education, believed they had a special connection to their land, that it was just as alive as they were, if not more so.

Another musical breeze caressed as the woman said, "Love Island." Her words sounded sung. "That's one name for our paradise."

"What's another? Like a more official name I might have seen on my boarding pass?"

"What's wrong with Love? It, or your view of it, is what brought you here, right?"

"Why would you think that?"

"It's what brings all travelers here."

"I guess I had a little too much fun on the way here. Alcohol must've clouded my brain. I just felt like I wanted a vacation—needed a vacation—and, well, here I am."

"By yourself. Not with a special someone. Just like all the others."

"Well, the resort is for singles, right? And judging from what I saw back on the beach, it seems more than a few people found a special someone or two—or even three or more—last evening." He hoped his debauchery had been limited to alcohol. "But, no—to your point, I'm sure I traveled here alone. Why wouldn't I? Women where I live, they're all too toxic, you know? So tired of dealing with them."

The woman frowned at him. "Toxic?"

"You know . . . They'll only go out to dinner with you if they're hungry. You do what you can to take them to the best restaurant you can afford, but then they barely even talk to you. They're too busy filling their mouths and tapping on their phones.

"I'm a VP at a bank, one of the big ones. Multinational. And, boy, don't the women know and act like it. They can smell it . . .

"I'm telling you . . . I took a woman I'd been courting, online and off, to a nice restaurant—not one where I'd be seen by any of my colleagues or superiors—but überclassy. I prayed she would dress the part, even sent her the links to the restaurant's site and a few reviews in the better publications so that she would take the hint. She didn't—showed up in jeans and a sweatshirt. But, fine, whatever, it was dark. And I enjoyed her company. *Had* been, until she asked if she could order two meals, one for her and one to take home to her son.

"Now, I'm all for kids. And I get it. Single mom leaving her child alone for the evening—or with a babysitter, essentially alone—to go out with some man that's not his father or even his uncle. She wants to soothe the child when she returns. She wants the kid to have a taste—literally—of the experience she had when she temporarily abandoned the kid. I get it. So I said no problem. Then she ordered the three most expensive damn things off the menu.

"Hell, she went off menu, ordering the priciest entrée then throwing in two high-priced add-ons. All of it multiplied by two."

"Sustenance is important," she said. "For the young and for the loving."

"No doubt. That's why I didn't say anything. Paid the check with a cheesy smile on my face. Saw her again. A few times. Things were going well enough so that when I thought I'd take a trip to Jamaica, I invited her. She said cool, but only if she could bring her ten-year-old. I was cool with that. Got them both plane tickets. First class. Got them their own suite and everything. We were having a wonderful time each day, until late in the evening, *each* evening, when I tried to get her to leave her suite for mine. She said she couldn't. Not while her child was in the same building. It wouldn't be respectful to him. Never mind he wouldn't see, hear, or know about any of it . . . Yeah, after the third time she laid this on me, I knew exactly what she meant about *respect.* More than fifteen thousand dollars, *wasted* . . .

"So many experiences like that. *So* many. So much *waste.* I guess I must've come here to get away from it all—all the toxic women and their bullshit."

"You must have."

"Romance," he snorted. "It's been danced to death, huh?"

"If you say so."

"Well, how about you? You're a beautiful woman. You've probably experienced your fair share of flings. And flings flung wrong. What would you say?"

"I'd say we've spent all this time in each other's company, and you have yet to ask me my name."

He winced. "I—"

"It's Kelsi."

"I apologize. It was rude of me, I know. My name is—"

"Hadrian."

"Yes. Yes, of course you would know already. Those that employ you—they make you memorize the names of visitors, right?"

"Something like that."

"Kelsi"—he placed a hand on her shoulder, stopping her —"listen to me, *please*." He glanced about, searching for potential eavesdroppers, as he lowered his voice. "I don't remember coming here. I don't know what kind of kinky place this is. But from what I've seen, what I've heard—and not heard—from you . . . Well, I sense you may be in some kind of trouble. If I can help you, assist you in any way . . ."

"Ah"—she smiled, tilting her head to the left—"my white knight."

"I'm serious. I have resources."

"Yes, I know. I am a woman, after all. I can *smell* what it is you have that I can use."

"Kelsi, I didn't mean you. Not women like you."

"Like me?"

"Listen, stop playing games. Please."

"No games, Hadrian. You want to know about me; I'll tell you." She gestured for him to follow her off the path, onto the grass. He hesitated but followed, seeing she had done it to let the pair who had been trailing them on the path continue on their way unhindered.

Kelsi stopped walking once they were equidistant from their path and the next one over. "We grow up quickly here." She kept her voice low. "Very quickly. Each of us falls under the guidance of a caretaker until we reach full maturity. I had the misfortune of having a caretaker who did not care for her duties. Considered them abhorrent and herself an abomination. But rather than drowning herself in the surrounding waters, as would have been right and proper, she lived on, attempting to poison the minds of those under her care, attempting to convert others to her way of thinking, enough so that they might turn on the island itself and poison it, killing the Giver-Receiver, the lover and sustainer of us all.

"The diseased caretaker, she still has some adherents. Some of them live on, somewhere on the island. Where exactly, I don't know. Or care. But she, she is subdued, uninfluential. And I live on, and I will continue to live on—happy, blissful, and thriving—doing my small part each cycle to help maintain our joyously pulsing lover."

These native girls . . . Their minds weren't right, and he was no therapist.

He wouldn't get through to Kelsi. He couldn't save anyone who didn't even understand their plight. Her position, her worldview—all normal to her. If he tried to do or say anything to rock it, the consequences could range from unpleasant to fatal. He didn't want to risk blood on his hands. Or a lawsuit. She felt she was happy, so best to leave her to her feelings. Best course for him was to just get to his room and work on trying to recover his memories, then decide whether to stay on or get the hell out of here.

"Okay"—he shrugged—"you say you're happy, and I take you at your word. Now, how much longer to the hotel?"

"Hotel?"

"Or whatever name you have for it here. My *dwelling*. I figured the party would've been a good way away from where we sleep, eat, and rest—but, Miss Kelsi, this has been quite a trek."

"We're almost there. Just over the hill."

Forgoing the path, they continued on grass, walking side by side up the gentle slope. He likely wouldn't have noticed the ground trending upward if she hadn't referred to a hill.

Neither said a word as they reached the top. Neither said a word as he stopped to gape at the spectacle downhill and Kelsi continued on.

She kept on for a dozen steps before looking back at him over her shoulder. "Coming?" He had no response.

No buildings or any other structures were in sight. Rather, down below, in a large area where there was no grass or plants, only dirt, dozens of men and women were paired off, nude or getting there. They engaged in passionate embraces—and more. A love-in. A mass love-in. *Some old-school hippie stuff*, he thought, *but with actually attractive people.* The groundskeepers and those they'd led to this spot were indulging in a spectacular orgy of two hundred or more.

He'd come to a pleasure island. One where he could lose himself with abandon.

His mind raced. Perhaps nothing had happened on the beach other than a form of foreplay, where the resort's guests had been plied with drinks—love potions mixed with sleeping potions—elixirs to prepare them for this.

It seemed silly. *Potions . . .*

Crazy, even.

But he couldn't dismiss what he was seeing.

"Hadrian?"

His gaze shifted to Kelsi. She was beaming. Wanton. He

took her in—all of her. Assessing her. Not as a beautiful woman who worked for a resort. Not as a potential victim of trafficking or exploited labor. But solely as a potential sexual partner.

"Yes—I'm coming."

He stumbled on his first couple of steps down the slope but recovered into a light jog toward her. Together, they descended at a quickened pace. Hadrian was only marginally aware that other pairs were doing the same, trickling in from the various other paths leading to this valley of delights.

Hadrian and Kelsi entered in among the congregation, eventually finding a space where there was ample room for them to ignore their surroundings and gaze into each other's eyes—*deeply*—for the first time. Her teal-green irises sent a shiver through him.

"There are many activities on the island," Kelsi said. "But this is the one I was born to perform."

She kissed him before he could make the move. Again, he shivered with pleasure, even as his legs felt as if they'd been jabbed with several needles.

He ignored the below-the-waist pain to reciprocate her boldness, pulling her closer, loosening or tightening his grip as necessary as his lips traveled beyond her face and neck.

Who was he to resist her? The woman was no victim. She'd said so. She'd insisted so. And this was why he'd come—wasn't it? It had to be the reason. Why else would he book a trip to such a resort? He'd been needing to let loose for a long time. And now was his time.

They discarded their garments and shared another kiss—a powerful meeting of thin layers of skin—lips pushing, pulsing, sinking into one another, releasing steam he heard and faintly saw while both bodies experienced a frisson of deep connection.

"Release the body," she murmured as they disengaged. "Twist the soul."

Blood rushed to his head as she kissed and tossed whispers, which he inhaled as commands—*demands* he'd no choice but to obey. Licking, nipping, biting . . . In return, she laid on him a constellation of pecks and sharp pinches.

As he moved his body this way and that, hers responded with sudden jerks and twists and other movements she rapidly fine-tuned as she became more and more familiar with him. Soon their bodies synced, moved as one, with steadily increasing speed.

He didn't know how and didn't care, but as he thrusted, she seemed to massage multiple areas across his body—smacking, punching, kneading, pulling handfuls of flesh and twisting. Pleasure intermingled with pain.

He didn't stop. *Couldn't.*

The intensity grew. His sight of the world outside his body left him, turned inward. He saw nothing but an orange-smeared darkness behind his eyes as he felt every cell—skin, blood, hair, organs, others—each particulate of himself transmogrifying into an ice crystal, a snowflake melting and refreezing every few seconds. Over and over and over.

As his consciousness fizzed, he was dimly aware his body was dissolving into foam.

———

KELSI'S BODY felt like a prickly plant—one showered with cold lights, dazzled in dark colors, and rapidly erupting with thousands of buds, each of them bursting to reveal the tiny ripe heads of newborn babies, screaming and welcoming the mass of winged things with sharp beaks darting in and out, drilling into their skulls, sipping, drinking the substances of the tiny ones' chaotic minds, unformed thoughts, out of which entire universes, a multitude of new realities might be spawned. She shrieked at the pain, cried her throat raw at the frightening visions she witnessed.

Engulfed in a peach-colored foam and trembling uncontrollably, she collapsed into the muck her coupling had made, the result of a soul dissolved into oblivion.

She'd done everything right. Her new techniques . . . Employing the sand flies . . . But the expected ecstasy had been corrupted. Elation had eluded her. She hadn't been enraptured but tortured and left confused. What in Euphoria's name had happened?

Catching her breath, she looked around. Her siblings sang and reveled, wrestling, plucking gobbets of muck from the ground and tossing them at one another, rubbing their own writhing bodies with it, before hugging, joining arms, their voices harmonizing into a greater, grander song, a tune destined to become one with the wind as the siblings began their trek from the field.

Kelsi joined them, but she did not sing. Her body ached. Her thoughts fogged her brain.

As she walked, however, putting more distance between her and the field, the internal haziness gradually cleared, revealing bits and pieces of images from another realm, another life.

She was born here, of the soil . . . But she was not from the island, not originally.

She'd come from the waters. Waters far from the shores of the island. But she hadn't been born there either. She'd met her end there. The ending of her first life.

She'd been on a craft—a large watercraft—with several others. Women and men. Many men. Wealthy men. Entitled men. Men like Hadrian. Men like the others with whom she'd coupled.

Some of these men wanted her. Her body. Only her body. She'd only wanted conversation. She'd wanted advice on how to advance a stalled career. One of the men made a promise, lured her away from the others.

She was grabbed, pushed, assaulted, *hurt*. First fighting off shock, she fought back. Harder, with everything she had. She tried to hurt back. She was overpowered.

She—her body—fell, was tossed, was discarded . . . She ended up in the waters, sinking. Into oblivion.

Until her rebirth on the island. From the soil, from the spilled blood of those who'd been sent to the island for punishment; those who'd been judged by higher powers to be worthy of no existence in any realm of reality; those who thought they were still fully alive but, in truth, had been stripped down and partially converted into an absorbable form. Their souls—destined to be dissolved, the process and aftermath of their dissolution helping keep Euphoria fertile so that it could continue to sustain its inhabitants. Its children. Its servants.

Was this where she belonged, or was her body—her body and her talents—just being used against her true will, manipulated for a purpose she didn't really understand? A purpose she couldn't understand because she'd failed to listen to anyone who might tell her what she didn't want to hear?

"A perfect climax should not be the goal of any young one— young in age or experience. It reveals truths one may not be ready to confront."

No. It wasn't so. It simply couldn't be.

Her old caretaker had tried and tried again to insert her false wisdom into Kelsi's head. One "off" experience with a drop, and suddenly, the old woman was in her head, taking up residence.

"*Hey*—everything okay?"

A few of her sisters and brothers stood in front of her with concerned expressions. She blankly stared back at them. She'd paid no attention to her surroundings as she'd been walking with them. She hadn't realized she'd stopped at the same point from which she'd broken away from them the day before. Her new ritual . . .

She'd come back to it later, when she had something to brag about.

"Yeah." She gently nodded her head. "*Yes*—everything will be okay."

Just one bad experience. It wouldn't be the end of her world. Her next coupling would be better. Maybe the best yet. She'd just have to try extra hard.

She continued on with her siblings toward the overlook. On the way, they waded through streams to cleanse their skin and clothes. The winds caressed them dry before they reached their destination.

By the time they were all spread out on the grass, clustered in groups—conversing, joking, and laughing—Kelsi's usual happiness and optimism had returned and remained firm.

A hush fell over them all when the winds changed. Everyone rose to their feet as sparkles flecked the clouds above.

Gradually, the points of light fell, a few at a time, their actual shape becoming more apparent as they descended.

Kelsi and her siblings watched—eyes wide, mouths agape— as the veiny spheres, dozens of them, fell from the dark skies, their ephemeral skins destined to burst open on the rocks at the edge of the island, releasing their oils and depositing their passengers . . . Lost men and women, once trapped in a fearfully dark personal reality, sustained by lies, living on ideas of love that were poisonous to the greater world in which they breathed and traveled. Their final destination was here: Euphoria.

The siblings lived to welcome the travelers. And, out of unquestionable love for the Giver-Receiver, Kelsi would do whatever she must to ensure the happiness and excitement she experienced in living only increased.

THANK YOU

Thank you for reading Blind Dates. If you enjoyed this volume, please remember to leave an online review and spread the word.

ABOUT THE AUTHOR

Harambee K. Grey-Sun writes in a variety of genres, but his stories often fall somewhere on the spectrum of horror, ranging from the supernatural to the psychological.

For more information:
www.harambeegreysun.com

BY HARAMBEE GREY-SUN

Poetry

Spring's Fall (Autumn Numbers * Book I)

Wine Songs, Vinegar Verses

Trinity & Its Twin

www.ingramcontent.com/pod-product-compliance
Lightning Source LLC
Chambersburg PA
CBHW070541100726
47907CB00004B/1214